Five
of Hearts

A SCALLOP SHORES NOVEL

JENNIFER DECUIR
author of *Drawn to Jonah*

CRIMSON
ROMANCE

F+W Media, Inc.

Published by
Crimson Romance
an imprint of F+W Media, Inc.
10151 Carver Road, Suite 200
Blue Ash, OH 45242. U.S.A.
www.crimsonromance.com

ISBN 10: 1-4405-7959-8
ISBN 13: 978-1-4405-7959-2
eISBN 10: 1-4405-7960-1
eISBN 13: 978-1-4405-7960-8

Cover art © 123rf.com/curaphotography

To my parents:
Not a day goes by that I don't miss you both and wish I could share this exciting new chapter in my life with you. Until we see each other again … I love you.

Acknowledgments

Many thanks to my wonderful friend, Sriya, for beta reading each chapter and answering my weird questions about growing up in a family of multiples.

Thank you to Jessica and Beata, my newest "fans" and tireless cheerleaders.

I am honored to have your support.

CHAPTER ONE

"Running away" was such a cowardly term. Dean preferred to think of it as "permanently relocating." Lying back, he breathed in a gulp of fresh Maine air, laced with pine and beach roses and the sharp tang of the Atlantic Ocean. He felt his muscles relax, really relax, as he sank deeper into the hammock. He'd waited almost half his life for this.

At fourteen years old, Dean had willingly forfeited his anonymity—and the peace and quiet that went with it—for the chance to become an internationally revered pop star. He'd become Dino Valentine, lead singer of the boy band Five of Hearts. For the next six years, Dean's life had been a whirlwind of recording sessions, hours of choreography, concert dates, and appearances.

Fame. Fortune. The perks that came with being a household name. It all sounded great in the beginning, but no one ever told him about the downside of being under the microscope. All the people who wanted their share of the pie, their moment in the spotlight, their chance to spend someone else's hard earned money. And the devious ways they plotted to get it.

In the six years since the band had broken up, Dean had kept to himself as much as possible, and tried to stay out of the public eye. He didn't leave his Malibu mansion except to go visit his band mates. He was content to spend his days writing music, swimming laps in the pool, and chasing off opportunistic photogs looking for the chance to catch Dean in a compromising position—the money shot that would set them up for life.

Now, in the midst of yet another groundless paternity suit, Dean knew he needed to go where the money-grubbing vultures couldn't find him. He was done with the life of a celebrity. He was done with Southern California.

He swung from the hammock in his new backyard, a plate of cookies and an ice cold beer within reach. His baseball cap was pulled low over his eyes to block out the glare of the sun. A group of tall arborvitae bushes hid the next house from view, giving Dean the illusion that he was truly alone, something he'd been craving for so long. He opened the book in his lap but stared at the words, unseeing. He hoped all these changes, the cross-country move, and buying a new house, would bring him the sense of peace that had been missing.

Several years ago, Dean had had a tutor who came from Maine. He'd listen for hours while the man talked about what a beautiful state it was. He'd hailed from the coast and spent summers helping on his dad's lobster boat. He had told Dean all about the snowmobiling, the ice fishing, bonfires, and parties in the woods. He'd described the crisp tang of autumn in the air and the riot of color from the trees, almost the entire month of October. There was something to do all year round.

Dean closed his eyes and breathed deeply of the fresh mown grass, ocean breezes, and a flowering shrub he couldn't put a name to. He dug a toe into the lawn and set his hammock gently swinging. Smacking his lips, he grinned in drowsy happiness. He was falling asleep in the middle of the day. What a foreign concept that had become. Dean pillowed his head on his arm and snuggled into the hammock for some rest. Just as he was drifting off he thought he heard giggling.

Cracking one eye open, Dean scanned the yard. There, over by the blueberry bushes, was a carrot-topped little pixie. He shook his head, opening his other eye, and looked again. This time the tiny child was over by the willow tree, crouched down and grinning. Dean rubbed his eyes and leaned out of the hammock for a better look. Wait. Now the little thief was right beside him—stealing his cookies! How could he be everywhere at once?

Dean reached out to grab him by the collar but forgot he was in the hammock and lost his balance. The miniature con artist screeched as Dean nearly fell on top of him. He took off, a cookie in each hand. Dean landed with a thud on the lawn.

"Hey, get back here with my cookies!" Dean tried to get up to run after the child but tripped over his own feet and landed face first in the turf, knocking his ball cap off his head.

"Problems?" A soft, feminine voice, thickly laced with humor, called from the edge of the lawn.

Dean stood, brushing his clothes off. He was starting to think chasing off paparazzi was preferable to chasing after … was it only a child? So much for peace and quiet.

"That kid made off with my cookies." He scanned the perimeter of the yard, unable to locate the cookie thief.

"That team works fast. I imagine your cookies have been gobbled up by now." He could actually hear the amused smile in her voice.

That team? There was more than one? Dean was starting to get a headache.

"How'd you all get into my yard anyway?" Rubbing his temples, he tried to work out how he'd thought there was one kid darting through his shrubs only to find there were more. How many more? This was confusing.

"There is a break in the hedge. I have a finely tuned radar when it comes to this bunch. I had a feeling they were up to no good."

Frowning, Dean snatched up the empty plate. He turned, finally prepared to square off with this latest intruder. His words stuck to his tongue. His gaze was drawn to a pair of startlingly blue eyes. A light breeze picked up a strand of her long red hair, tossing it around playfully. Red hair and freckles. Suddenly, he was back in grade school remembering his first crush. Oh, he was a goner.

She smiled, shrugging her shoulders in apology. The twinkle in her eyes called the sincerity of the apology into question, yet somehow Dean didn't mind.

"My name is Shannon. I live next door with those ... cookie thieves."

"I, um, I'm Dean." His brain was working overtime, trying to catch up. "Just how many kids are running around here?"

"Brady, Brenna, and Brian, you march those little butts out here right this second!"

Dean watched in horror as not one, but three little children peered out from behind the tall hedge and proceeded to line up in front of Shannon for inspection. He didn't know much about kids, but he'd guess them to be about four or five years old. Their heads were bowed but Dean could tell they weren't the least bit repentant. There were cookie crumbs on their cheeks and they looked to be trying very hard not to giggle.

Grudgingly, he had to admit they were cute—for thieving little cookie heathens. The little girl, Brenna, looked him right in the eye and winked. Dean focused on his sneakers, trying not to let the munchkin charm him.

"What do you have to say for yourselves?" Shannon eyed them all, her face stern, and her features grim.

"We're sorry, mister," they offered in unison. Dean doubted that was the first time they'd had to apologize for something like this.

"It's okay, I guess. You owe me some new cookies, though." He folded his arms across his chest and cast a forlorn glance at the empty plate. He really had been looking forward to those cookies.

"That's right, kiddos. You are going to spend tomorrow afternoon in the kitchen with me. No outdoors time until we get a nice batch of ... " She offered him an opening.

"Chocolate chip—no nuts."

"Right. You all will be baking chocolate chip cookies, with no nuts, for Mr. Dean. You will not cut through the gap in the bushes to deliver them, but will instead use the walkway, like civilized neighbors."

Shannon silenced the groans of disappointment with a single look. Dean was impressed. She sent the children on their way back to their own yard and turned to him. He stood still while she gave him the once over, his nerves on edge as he waited to see if she'd recognize him. He panicked, reaching up to his bare head, when he realized he wasn't wearing his hat. He always wore a hat.

Shannon looked like she was in her mid-twenties, just the right age to have been a fan when Five of Hearts was at the top of their fame. If she recognized him, it would blow any chance of his hiding out in blessed anonymity in this quaint seaside town. Instead, she merely ducked her head shyly and played with the hem of her shirt. Whew. Maybe he was in the clear.

"Sorry about that heathen crack. They're cute kids. Are they triplets? You must be the older sister, then."

"Thank you … to the cute kids *and* to the older sister bit. That wasn't necessary. Totally welcome, mind you, but not necessary. Nope, they're all mine." She blushed.

"Wow. I can't even imagine one kid, but three at once? What did your husband say when you guys found out you were having triplets?"

"In a word? Goodbye." Shannon shrugged, feigning indifference. "Let's just say he didn't find himself up to the challenge."

"What a slimeball!" Dean clapped a hand over his mouth, embarrassed that he'd let that judgment be voiced aloud.

What kind of man would abandon his children? It was something Dean had been accused of many times—but something he would never do, if a child were actually his.

Dean hadn't been quite seventeen years old when he was named in his first paternity suit. He hadn't been an angel, but he'd been careful. His manager had drilled it into all of them just how important it was to use protection. Dean had known the girl was lying. And yet he'd been advised to settle out of court, pay the girl what she wanted, and keep it out of the news.

But when this latest paternity suit surfaced, he knew he couldn't keep paying off these women and hoping the problem would just go away. He needed to take a stand, and stop the madness once and for all.

Shannon's trill of laughter was music to his ears.

"Eh, I like to look at it as him doing us a favor." Shannon turned toward the opening in the hedge. "Listen, I'm really sorry the kids invaded your space like this. It's just that they were used to playing over here. The house has been on the market for years. This just kind of became an extension of our backyard. I'll try to keep them out of here in the future."

"Yeah, okay." Dean watched her duck her head and pass through the tight space in the bushes.

This new life was not shaping up to be the tranquil escape he'd been looking for. He'd sworn off women—especially women that showed up on his doorstep with a child. Triplets! Screw the Arborvitae. He was going to have to build a fence. A really tall one.

Dean went back to his hammock and tried again to take that nap. If he heard sweet harp music in the background, he paid it no heed. He dreamed of tiny pixies with crumbs on their cheeks surrounding a beautiful fairy queen with gossamer wings and long, bright red hair.

• • •

The three little cookie thieves had been fed, bathed, and sent to bed early for stealing from their new neighbor. Shannon should have welcomed the extra quiet time but she found herself restless, unable to relax. Normally able to calm her racing brain with nimble fingers, she was frustrated when crocheting didn't seem to work. She set the afghan-in-progress aside.

Heading to her cozy little kitchen, Shannon stood on tiptoe and tried to catch a glimpse of the big house next door. She could just make out a twinkle or two of lights through the thick hedging as her new neighbor settled in for the evening. Dean. His name was Dean.

Dust flew as she drew her curtains closed for the first time, not for privacy but to shut out the obsessive thoughts that had been plaguing her since she'd met the annoyingly hot Malibu Ken lookalike that afternoon. Seriously, the guy must have come from Southern California, with that deep tan. Did he surf all day? How did he afford one of the luxury summer homes in Scallop Shores? Screenwriter? Actor? He didn't look like anyone she'd ever seen in the movies. But then again, when was the last time she'd been to the movies? It must have been at least five years.

It was a cool evening in her tiny little caretaker's cottage, behind the huge summer house of her employer, Ms. Sheffield. Shannon perched on the edge of a wooden chair at the table. She wrapped her fingers around the mug of tea she'd fixed and stared down into the whirling steam. It was May and things were starting to get busier in the little tourist town of Scallop Shores, Maine. Ms. Sheffield would probably make an appearance over the holiday weekend. Shannon needed to get the big house ready for her arrival.

She'd be eternally grateful to the wealthy Wall Street mogul who had taken a chance on a very pregnant, single mom, who had never even been to college. Ms. Sheffield had never married, never had children, so Shannon had been flummoxed when the old woman took them under her wing. Last spring, after the muddy season was over, she'd had a huge play area built in the backyard, with swings and a slide, a sandbox, and a climbing wall. Shannon had offered to have it taken out of her paycheck, a little each week, but Ms. Sheffield wouldn't hear of it.

But the successful businesswoman was in her seventies now, and the weekends she hosted at her summer home were getting fewer and farther between. What would happen if she sold the place? Or worse, what if she died? She didn't have family to leave it to. Where did that leave Shannon and her kids? She'd gotten too comfortable with their easy life. She didn't have a back-up plan.

Agitated, Shannon carried her tea to the sink and dumped it out. She quickly rinsed the mug and set it in the drying rack. Tapping her fingers on the edge of the counter she looked around for some busy work. The counters were clean. The stove, oven, and refrigerator were spotless. She headed for the living room, certain to have something to do there. The Legos were all neatly put away. Brenna's tea set was on its tray, all the pieces together. Not even a stray sock lying on the floor. She blew out a long sigh and pursed her lips.

She wasn't usually on edge like this. Rolling her shoulders to try to work out some of the tension, Shannon trod quietly down the hall. She peeked her head around the half-open door to Brenna's room. One leg hung off the bed and her monkey was clutched tightly to her side. Shannon slipped in and slid the skinny leg back beneath the covers.

Across the hall, the boys slept in twin beds, side by side, a Batman nightlight in between. Brian snored softly while Brady muttered in his sleep. Shannon felt that familiar clutch in her heart, that same one she'd experienced for the first time as she held each of her new babies. It had never been her intention to raise such a large family alone. But life didn't always work out the way you would expect. Shannon learned the hard way that she didn't need a man.

The fact that a man just happened to have moved into the house that had been vacant as long as she'd lived here should not have rattled her the way it did. So what if he was good looking? Big deal that he could be about her age. They were polar opposites and she'd do well to remember that. Mr. Perfect Dean was some sort of trust fund baby and she was a glorified maid. She didn't need a man. She didn't need a neighbor who happened to be a man.

Disgusted that she was putting way too much thought into this, Shannon headed back down the hall—to scrub her perfectly clean kitchen.

CHAPTER TWO

"So then he just takes the plate of cookies, thanks us, and shuts the door!" Shannon threw her hands up in the air and let them fall back down again, slapping against her legs.

"You sure you didn't catch him at a bad time? Maybe he had a guest. What was he wearing when he came to the door?"

Shannon laughed as her friend Talia wiggled her eyebrows suggestively. Taking a peek through the office window, she could see the kids in the main play area of Tumble Tots. The instructor had given everyone scarves to dance with and they were having a ball. Shannon found her mug on the mug tree and helped herself to some coffee. She settled in at the desk with a sigh.

"It's not like I want to date the guy. My kids are doing just fine without a father figure." She took a sip and let the heat from the brew slide all the way down, warming her insides. "It just gets so quiet up there. I was hoping for someone to talk to, a little adult conversation once in a while."

"You're welcome to bring the squirts by any time you want, you know? Once a week can't be enough for your active bunch."

"This is my weekly treat. It's something to look forward to. And yes, once a week is plenty." Shannon smiled gratefully at the woman who had come to be a very dear friend.

There was no way Shannon could have afforded classes for the triplets at Tumble Tots. But one day, during story time at the library, she'd been approached by another mother of multiples. Talia and her husband owned Tumble Tots and she'd suggested it as a great way for the triplets to get their wiggles out and for Shannon to get out of the house. Embarrassed, Shannon had explained she didn't have the money to cover the cost of tuition. Talia had that part covered.

While the children attended the hour-long class in the play area, Shannon could help out Talia in the office. She'd do a little bookwork, some filing, envelope stuffing, anything was helpful. Some days she did help out. Most days, however, the two women holed up in the office with a pot of coffee and chatted. Talia had two-year-old twin boys. She totally understood what it was like to parent multiples. But since Shannon was getting these classes for free, she would not take advantage by bringing in her children more than the once a week they had agreed upon.

"I say give the guy the benefit of the doubt. Maybe he's shy. Maybe he's just not used to kids and doesn't know how to act around them."

"Yeah, he's definitely got a story. I mean, who just up and moves to a mansion on an isolated stretch of beach in Maine? He's young. Maybe not twenty-four, like me, but not much older. It's like he's hiding away."

"And if I know you, you aren't going to stop until you figure it out." Talia held up a finger, checked to make sure no one was going to walk in on them, and pulled a tin of cookies out of a desk drawer. "You never saw these, okay? I promised myself I'd lose ten pounds before bikini season."

"Cookies? What cookies?" Shannon snatched one out of the tin and grinned. "Maybe I'll send the kids over to play in his yard and feign innocence when he happens upon them."

"Wicked woman! You make me proud." The two women laughed over their coffee and cookies.

• • •

Dean stood on the wide front porch of the cottage on the other side of the hedges. He couldn't call first; he didn't have her number. He wasn't even sure what he was doing here in the first place. He'd tried to wait until the kids were probably in bed. But did Shannon go to bed early too? Heck, if he had three little ones running ragged on him all day, he probably would.

He leaned to the side and snuck a look in the window. There was a crack where the curtains didn't quite meet and he could see Shannon sitting in a huge, overstuffed chair. She appeared to be alone. Great. Now he was a stalker. Disgusted with himself, Dean almost turned to leave. The Tupperware container under his arm slipped and almost fell from his grasp. Blowing out a puff of air, he squeezed his shoulders together, stood up straighter, and knocked softly on the wooden door.

Footsteps scuffed louder the closer they came. The door opened a sliver and Dean could barely make out a flash of coppery hair and one narrowed blue eye. He held out the Tupperware, whether in defense or in explanation he wasn't certain. The eye he could see through the space in the door widened and the door was opened all the way.

"Hey, I wanted to return your cookie … thing." God, that was lame!

"No problem. You just scared me, is all. I'm not used to anyone knocking on my door at 8:30 at night. Guess I need to remember we're not alone up here on this road anymore."

"I didn't wake anyone, did I?"

"No, not at all. The kids went to bed an hour ago." She took the container from Dean but didn't appear as though she had any intention of inviting him in. He probably deserved that.

"Okay, well, I don't want to keep you up … "

"Don't be silly. It's early." She stole a glance behind her. "I don't want to wake them up. Would you like to sit out here on the porch with me? It's warm enough." Without waiting for an answer, she snagged a long, wool cardigan off a coat tree by the door and slipped outside.

Shannon settled on the porch swing, drawing her long legs up underneath her. Though there was plenty of room left on the swing, Dean chose a wicker chair in the corner. It creaked when he sat down.

"I didn't offer you anything to drink. I'm so sorry. What can I get you?"

"Oh, I don't need anything. Don't worry about it." Dean played with his fingers in his lap. He hadn't pictured this scene playing out quite like this. In his plan, he'd be halfway back to his own house already.

"No, really, I insist." Shannon untangled her limbs and stepped from the swing. "I'll be right back."

Dean watched the moths hovering around the porch light while he waited for his new neighbor to return. They reminded him of teenaged girls, autograph books in hand, jockeying for a close enough position around their favorite idol. He jerked his gaze away from the fluttering and wiped his palms on the fabric of his jeans. Before long, his hostess returned.

"So, what do you think of Maine? It *is* safe to assume you aren't from around here?" Shannon's voice issued from somewhere behind a tray, a large carafe hiding most of her face. "You don't have the look of a New Englander." She set the tray down on the wicker coffee table between them and poured hot chocolate into two cups.

Not bothering to ask what a New Englander was supposed to look like, Dean chuckled. "Let me guess… surfer dude?" He smiled at her embarrassed expression. "I get that a lot. And, no, I don't even know how to surf." He reached for the mug painted in tiny pink flowers, figuring the "#1 Mom" cup was meant for Shannon.

He leaned back in his chair, took a big swallow, and breathed in the sweet smell of late spring. There was still a slight chill to the air after dark, but surely that wouldn't be for much longer.

"Maine comes highly recommended. I have a laundry list of things I'm supposed to experience, according to a tutor I had years ago." He leaned forward, his brows knitted together as he shook his head. "Maybe you can help me out with something. What is a whoopie pie? Seriously, is that even for real?"

Shannon's laugh was so sweet, he couldn't help but smile.

"Absolutely. Whoopie pies are for real, and you definitely need to experience one." She licked her lips and closed her eyes for a moment. "Maybe I'll just bake up a batch for you."

"Cookies, cocoa, whoopie pies … you're going to make me fat."

"Well, the great thing about Maine is that I can show you the best places to swim, awesome hiking trails, and beautiful, scenic bike rides."

She looked so excited at the prospect that warning bells were starting to go off in Dean's brain. Oh, why did she have to be so damned adorable? She had her knees drawn up close and her cocoa resting on top of them. She wiggled her fuzzy purple slipper-clad toes on the edge of her seat.

He wondered, yet again, if there was any way she had recognized him as the front man for Five of Hearts and was somehow keeping the knowledge to herself. To what end? Dean hated to admit that he just couldn't figure this woman out. He must have waited too long to say something because she was watching him closely, a sad smile on her face.

"You didn't come to Maine for whoopie pies. You came here to be alone." It wasn't a question, and from the look on her face, she didn't expect to be told any differently.

"It's nothing personal." God, did that come out as lame as he thought it had? Dean chanced a quick look at Shannon and she was still watching him, that sad little smile threatening to put a chink in the fortress he'd spent years building up.

"I just wanted a chance at a new life, a new beginning. My life before … it was crazy. It wasn't me, wasn't what I wanted. They wouldn't leave me alone." Too much! He'd said too much! Dean looked up sharply, wanting desperately to get inside Shannon's head and find out what she knew.

"You want to go it alone. Dean, look at me. If anyone gets your situation it's me."

"Well, that's part of it, yeah." He set his mug down on the tray, his eyes straying to the porch steps. An overpowering urge to escape had him drumming his fingertips restlessly on his knees.

"You also want to *be* alone. You bought that isolated house surrounded by nothing but summer homes, so you could hide away."

Again, she'd nailed it.

"All right, Doctor Shannon, what am I hiding from?" Dean's snarky remark was meant as a warning to back off. The truth hurt and he was scared of what her answer would be.

"I'm sorry," she whispered.

He hadn't been expecting that.

"It's none of my business and I feel awful for making you uncomfortable."

Now it was his turn to feel like a heel. Dean shook his head.

"No, you didn't … it's just … " Suddenly, he was at a complete loss for words.

"Hey, I'm a big girl. It's fine." Shannon stood up and began to clear away their evening snack. "You go on back to your new house, your new life."

"I … thank you for the hot chocolate. You didn't have to go to all that trouble."

"That's what neighbors do for each other, Dean. They welcome new folks into their lives as friends." She lifted the tray and set it on her hip in order to open the front door.

"You're my new friend, Dean. Like it or not. I'll respect your need for privacy if that is what you really want … for now. But you've got to come out of your shell sooner or later. I can't wait to get to know you when you're ready."

And with that Shannon gently shut the door behind her. Dean was left standing on the porch more unsure and confused than he'd been when he had first stepped up here to drop off a cookie container. Dear God, that woman was a force to be reckoned with. He headed back to his own house. The idea of having privacy suddenly seemed bleak, not as satisfying as he'd imagined.

Heading up his own driveway, Dean frowned at the dark, unwelcoming windows. He remembered watching Shannon, curled up in a chair in her living room. The lamp light was cozy. She'd looked so comfortable. He knew the kids were snug in their beds. Now, that was a home.

No. That wasn't what he wanted. He wanted peace, quiet, days on end going by when he didn't see or hear from anyone. That was what he wanted. Wasn't it?

CHAPTER THREE

It had been raining for four days straight and Shannon was going out of her mind. She hadn't seen her new neighbor since he'd shown up on her porch five nights ago. She'd promised to give him the privacy he craved and she would keep that promise. Her two little boys streaked by, hollering as they ran. Shannon raised her eyes to the ceiling, choosing not to ask why they were not wearing a stitch of clothing.

"Mommy, Rosie is playing hide and seek and I can't find her. Can you tell her it's time to come out now? I think maybe she wants a snack." Brenna, no doubt feeling outnumbered by her brothers, had recently invented an imaginary friend.

"It's nearly lunchtime, Bren. Rosie will come out when she gets tired of hiding." Shannon plucked a tee shirt off the coffee table and a small pair of jeans off the arm of the couch.

Brenna sighed dramatically and raced off to her next adventure. Shannon snatched a pair of Superman underwear from the top of the television, carrying her growing pile of discarded clothing with her as she went. She was just passing the front door when a knock nearly made her drop everything. She took a calming breath and answered the door. The sight of Dean on her front porch made her heart beat just a bit faster. Too late, she wished she'd ditched the pile of laundry in her arms so she could pat down her messy hair.

"Well, hello there, neighbor. What brings you out on this miserable day?"

"Does it rain like this often? I feel like I'm in Seattle," Dean groused, his hands shoved deep in his pockets.

"Aw ... not used to the wet stuff, huh? Wait until the snow is so high you can't even make it over here, unless you have snowshoes." Shannon chuckled at the look of horror on Dean's face. She held the door wide and announced, "Come on in, take off your clothes and join the party!"

Dean had been stepping over the threshold when she said this and he stopped and looked down at her. Her face heated, partly from embarrassment and partly from the intense way he was looking at her. It was like he already knew what she'd look like without her clothes ... and he liked what he saw.

"Sorry, that came out all wrong. The boys have decided to boycott clothing today. I'm not sure what the game is." Shannon put as much distance between them as possible, ignoring the way certain parts of her body felt as though they were waking up from a long sleep.

"Sounds fun." His voice was a sexy purr.

"Come on into the kitchen." She fought the urge to fan herself with her hand. "I'd love a little non-pre-K conversation."

Shannon headed across the hall and tried not to picture Dean checking out her butt as he followed behind. *Geez! Head out of the gutter, Fitzgerald! Of course he's not checking out your butt.* She chanced a peek over her shoulder to reassure herself. He was! She almost stumbled over her own feet.

"I'm not interrupting anything, am I?" Dean pulled out a chair at the dining room table in the breakfast nook and prepared to sit down.

"No! Mr. Dean, stop!" Brenna ran up to him, shaking her head, her eyes as wide as saucers. "You almost sat on Rosie." She pulled out a different chair and motioned for him to sit in that one instead.

Shannon stifled a grin, first at the apologetic look on Dean's face and then as that look turned to confusion. He shook his head as he studied the chair he nearly sat in. He glanced from the chair to the little girl and back again.

"I think Rosie must have jumped out when she saw me coming."

"She's still there. You scared her." Rust red pigtails swung jauntily as the five-year-old jutted out her chin and put her hands on her hips.

Uh oh! Shannon knew that stance. Her bored little girl was looking for an argument. For a split second she considered waiting it out, seeing how Dean would handle himself in an argument to prove the existence of an imaginary person. Nah. She was bored, too, and if she let Brenna spout off, Dean would probably go running back to his self-imposed isolation.

"Hey, baby, why don't you go round up your brothers and tell them we're doing something special for lunch." Shannon dropped a kiss on her daughter's head as she skipped toward the doorway. "And make sure they are at least wearing underwear!"

"This is a bad time. I didn't mean to barge in when you were fixing lunch." Dean's gaze went past Shannon, scanning the kitchen counter. Perhaps looking for a hint as to what was to be served?

"Yes. Yes, you did. And I'm glad you came." Shannon wasn't trying to tease. She really was happy he'd stopped by ... no matter the reason.

Dean's attention had returned to the wooden chair he had almost sat in. He scratched his head, opened his mouth like he was going to speak, and then shut it again. Shannon checked to make sure Brenna was off on her chore and then strode to the supposedly occupied chair and planted herself in it. She kept all traces of humor from her face while she looked up at Dean.

"I'm really missing something here, aren't I?" Dean wrinkled up his nose. "She doesn't have a pet bug or something, does she?"

Now she could no longer hold it in. Shannon burst out laughing.

"No, silly." She dabbed at her eyes. "Rosie is her imaginary friend." She lowered her voice. "She's new around here. We're all still getting used to her."

Impulsively, she reached out and patted Dean's hand. He didn't snatch it away, though she wondered how much willpower it took for him to remain still. Their eyes met and just as quickly they both chose something different to focus their attention on. Shannon cleared her throat and got up from the table.

"It's been a miserable few days, huh?" She busied herself getting lunch fixings out of the fridge.

"Yeah, miserable." Dean's voice was gruff. Was he talking about the weather, like she had been, or something else?

"I thought we could have a picnic … on the living room floor. What do you think?"

"Eat on the floor?"

"No, we'll eat on our picnic blanket. We're missing out on some prime picnic weather with the rain as steady as it's been."

"I can't remember the last time I've been on a picnic." He appeared deep in thought. "And I don't think I have ever had an indoor picnic before."

"Aren't you glad you came over, then?"

● ● ●

Dean's idea had been successful … just not in the way he had figured. He sat awkwardly, a paper plate perched precariously on his crossed legs. On either side of him sat a carrot topped little boy. One wore only underwear and a superhero cape. The other wore swim trunks and a cowboy vest. Had he dressed so foolishly when he was that age? Doubtful.

Shannon leaned over and spooned more potato salad onto his plate. Dean looked down in surprise.

"Omigosh, I'm so sorry. I'd probably be in your face, cutting your meat if we were eating dinner at the table. Guess I'm in mommy-mode 24/7." She scooted back over to her corner of the picnic blanket and began to nibble on a carrot stick. Dean liked how her cheeks bloomed bright pink and how the blush crept down her neck.

"It's fine. I was just going to ask for seconds anyway."

"Mr. Dean, do you have any kids?" One of the boys, he couldn't remember who was who, placed a sticky palm on Dean's khakis and cocked his head to the side, waiting for an answer.

"No!" Dean blinked. He hadn't meant for it to come out quite so emphatically. "I don't have any children. People have children when they're married. I'm not married, so ... no children." Did he sound as defensive as he thought? He snuck a look at Shannon and nearly groaned when he realized how intently she was following his answer.

"Mommy's not married and she has kids. Three of us. Triplets." Now the other little boy had chimed in. Thankfully, this one kept his messy hands to himself.

"But once upon a time, your mommy used to be married, right?" Dean bit his tongue, realizing, too late, that he knew nothing about Shannon's past and had no right to make any assumptions. He winced, wishing he could take back his words.

"Of course," she coughed out. She pounded a small fist against her sternum like she had gotten something caught in her throat. Ah, yes ... touchy subject. Fine by him. Relationships were the last thing he wanted to discuss.

They finished up their picnic with very little conversational input from the adults. Brenna put on an impromptu puppet show with the raspberries she'd stuck to the tops of her fingers. The boys held a mock sword fight with fried chicken drumsticks. Dean waited for Shannon to intervene and was mildly surprised when she only laughed at their antics. When the triplets were done eating, everyone helped to clean up the mess and carry it into the kitchen to either throw away or wash.

"That would not be acceptable behavior in a restaurant." Shannon threw the words out over her shoulder as she stood at the sink. The kids had wandered out of the room so she must have been speaking to him. "But I find that if I give them the opportunity to be silly at the occasional mealtime, then they're pretty well behaved on the whole."

"It must be so hard to raise all three by yourself. Do you have any help at all?" Dean carried the empty potato salad bowl to the sink and plunged it into the sudsy water Shannon had filled it with.

"My mom comes out a few times a year, stays for a couple of weeks. But she's got her own life. She's so busy." She smiled up at him.

"Man, if I had kids I'd definitely need backup." Dean grabbed the dishtowel and intercepted a plate before Shannon could set it in the rack to air dry.

"What are you doing? Go sit down. I can do this." Her hands fluttered as she tried to grab the plate back.

"You fed me lunch. The least I can do is help clean up the dishes." He held up a hand when he saw she was about to argue with him. "You're not asking for help, okay? I get it. I'm helping anyway, and you are going to have to deal with it." He held her gaze until she relented.

Shannon shrugged her shoulders noncommittally and scrubbed the tines of a fork. She kept her attention focused on the sink in front of her. Dean reached for another plate to dry and tried to ignore the growing need to help this woman. Clearly, she didn't want help and she seemed to have a handle on things. So why did he feel this intense desire to be her knight in shining armor?

They finished the rest of the dishes in silence. Dean watched the rain slide down the windowpane in wriggling rivulets. It was wet and miserable out there. He'd worked himself into a nasty mood this morning, upon waking to the same dreary weather that he felt had gone on for weeks. Munching on dry cereal, about the only food left in the house, had not improved things. Out of desperation he had found himself on Shannon's doorstep. Now he worried that this might become something of a habit.

The triplets were playing quietly in the living room. Had he really thought of them as hooligans before? Dean felt bad. It wasn't that he had anything against children. Kids were cute—generally. It was the being forced to assume financial responsibility for children he knew weren't his that turned him off.

He thought back to the certified letter sitting on his desk at home. A vein began to throb in his temple and he had to work his jaw around when he realized how hard he'd been clenching it.

"Do you have to head right home?"

"What?" Wrapped in his thoughts, Dean jerked slightly when Shannon tugged the dishtowel from his hands.

"I thought I could put on a movie. It's a good day for a movie."

Oh, yeah. He could definitely see himself getting more and more comfortable with spending time with the neighbor. This wasn't good. It wasn't what he needed. He needed space, lots and lots of space. And peace. Dean looked down into those calming blue eyes and knew he was falling. He'd agree to almost anything if she'd just keep looking at him like that.

No! That's how it always started. They lured him in with sweet smiles and soft gazes. They just wanted to spend time with him, they said. "Let's get to know each other." Then it was all about "'What did you bring me today?" and "I'm bored, let's go out." The latter meaning either they would find a way to spend lots of his money or he would be dragged to another exclusive party and be forced to make introductions.

"I need to go." Dean pivoted quickly and headed for the foyer without further explanation.

He stopped at the door and glanced briefly at the doorway to the living room. Should he say goodbye to the triplets? Would it be rude if he didn't? Shannon stood to the side and didn't say a word. She just watched him. Taking a deep breath, Dean edged closer to the doorway before he lost his nerve.

"Um, I'm heading out. I'll see you guys ... and lady ... around, huh?" He waggled his fingers then stuffed his hands in his pockets. Quick as a wink, three coppery-headed blurs came at him. Dean had just enough time to correct his stance before they knocked him to the ground. Instinctively, his arms came out to steady them. It ended up looking like a group hug. What should have felt awkward and uncomfortable, instead, felt more like a punch to the gut. They were hugging him goodbye. And he liked it. Oh, God, he was in more trouble than he'd thought.

CHAPTER FOUR

Grocery shopping was never fun. Grocery shopping with five-year-old triplets who wanted to be anywhere else but the supermarket was a nightmare. Armed with her detailed list, the sale flyer, an envelope full of coupons, and all the patience she could muster, Shannon hurried up and down the aisles. The sooner they finished shopping, the sooner they could all go out and play.

Turning a corner without looking, Shannon winced when her cart bounced hard off another. She did a quick head count and saw that all the kids were fine. She then focused her attention on the poor customer she'd nearly plowed down. He wore a ball cap low over dark sunglasses. Blonde, sun-streaked strands snuck out below the cap. He looked around furtively, like he was trying to hide from someone.

"Dean? Is that you? I'm so sorry I ran into you like that." Shannon angled her head, eyeing him quizzically.

"Uh. Hey. What's up?" He checked over his shoulder and hunched further into his lightweight jacket.

"You okay?" She was starting to get worried. He looked as though he were being stalked.

"I'm fine. I'm shopping … for food." He was clearly distracted.

"Run out of dry cereal, did you?"

"Yeah, I … how'd you know that?" He finally stood a little straighter and appeared to relax some.

"I figured you came by for lunch the other day because you were out of food. Or you were sick of your own cooking."

Sparing a quick peek in his grocery cart, Shannon quickly ruled out the "own cooking" part. Dean was certainly stocking up on the dry cereal … and cans of soup … bread … peanut butter. Oh, this was just so wrong! Even a bachelor could live better than this.

Hadn't his mother taught him to cook? Did he go out and buy new clothes whenever it was time to do laundry, too? Good grief!

"What's your favorite food?" She shot Dean a straight look that showed him she wasn't just making idle conversation.

"I don't know ... pizza?" He shrugged his shoulders, the gesture sliding him further into his jacket, like a turtle retreating into its shell.

"Come on. You're at a restaurant with a menu in front of you. What do you order?"

"Shannon, I really should hurry. I've got a ton of things to do back at the house." Again, he looked over his shoulder like he expected someone to be following him. His eyes darted everywhere at once and sweat was starting to bead on his upper lip.

He looks really freaked out, Shannon thought. He couldn't have been here long, and must have had more shopping to do. But he was in an awful hurry to get away. What could have him so worked up? Then it hit her, and Shannon had to refrain from slapping her forehead in discovery.

Dean was agoraphobic. All the evidence pointed to it. He lived alone and didn't want anyone around. He found it difficult to leave the house. Once out of it he couldn't stay away long before he felt too uncomfortable and had to rush back to the safety of his sanctuary. Oh, the poor man. Shannon had read articles on this condition and could only imagine the hell he must have to go through just to survive the day.

"Oh, my goodness, I am so sorry we kept you. You go on home and we'll catch up with you another time." Shannon gathered the children around her so Dean could maneuver his cart past them all. He paused just before he turned the corner of the aisle.

"It's nothing personal. I didn't want you to think ..." His words were a whispered mumble. He looked conflicted, one half of his body turned away from them ready to run and the other half leaning forward like he wanted to stay and chat.

Shannon shook her head and waved goodbye, her smile sad. She would not get choked up here. She didn't want to have to explain to the triplets why she was so upset for Mr. Dean. She imagined he'd be mortified if he found out her kids knew about what plagued him.

But if he thought he was in this alone, he would definitely have to think again! He had neighbors now, and neighbors helped each other out. If he felt safest at home, then she was going to make sure he was as comfortable as possible. He didn't need to subsist on soup and peanut butter sandwiches. Shannon was going to teach Dean to cook.

"Come on, kids. I think we're going to need a second cart."

Hastily, shoving her grocery list and envelope of coupons into her purse, Shannon also had to scrap her usual buying strategies. She hadn't had to shop for one since ... no, come to think of it, she'd had never had to shop for just herself. She eyed the shelves and bins for staples that weren't likely to go to waste. Instead of family packs of meat, like she would normally buy, Shannon picked up the smaller packages.

Her attention lingered over the pricier cuts of steak. Something told her that Dean was no stranger to filet mignon, or maybe even caviar. But if she was going to show her new hermit friend how to cook for himself, he was going to learn on her budget.

Even the triplets were helpful, knowing they were on a special mission. No one was whining, hitting, or asking for sugary snacks. Oh, they were definitely getting a treat for being so cooperative today! Shannon herded her brood over to the laundry aisle and asked the children to sniff the boxes of dryer sheets and decide, as a group, which one they liked best. While their backs were turned, she quickly snatched a box of crayons and three coloring books from a shelf on the opposite side of the aisle. She hid them in the grocery cart, under a big bargain bag of cereal.

Saving the things she didn't absolutely need for another day, Shannon and the kids hurried through the checkout. They stepped outside, momentarily blinded by the sun finally making an appearance. Hearing her name hollered across the parking lot, Shannon looked up to see Talia and her twins, Drake and Danny.

"Hey, there!" Talia said. "We were just bringing some supplies over to Tumble Tots. Think I could borrow your gang for a couple of hours? We just got some new gym equipment and it really needs some hands-on testing."

"Oh, maybe another time. I've got to get our groceries put away and then I have stuff to drop off at the neighbor's." Shannon smiled gratefully, still rolling the cart toward her minivan.

"Here, let us help." Talia slipped her hands from each of the boys and made sure they were both holding on to Shannon's shopping cart. Five children edged Shannon out of the way and pushed the cart in the right direction.

"Please? You'd be doing me a huge favor." Talia gripped Shannon's arm and drew her just far away enough to be out of range of little ears. "Jeff is on me to have another baby. Like two-year-old twins aren't enough!"

"Well, why didn't you say so? Had I known, I would have fed them a ton of candy." The women laughed.

"Seriously … the place is closed. It's just Jeff and me with the kids. We'll get them nice and tuckered out. You go spend time with your new man."

"Okay, but he's just a friend."

"Honey, you tell yourself whatever you need to." Talia gathered her boys, with the promise that she'd meet them all at the kiddy gym in just a few minutes.

• • •

It was strange not having the triplets around. Shannon's first instinct was to let the guilt she felt over enjoying herself ruin the peaceful solitude of the moment. She was all about making sure she had plenty of "me time" after the kids went to bed, but this was different. It was daylight. She didn't have to pick them up for two hours, more if she needed it, Talia had assured her. It felt like playing hooky. It felt naughty. It felt good. Forget the guilt—this was too precious an opportunity to pass up!

Shannon smiled cheerily when Dean opened his door and gently nudged her way past him with her arms loaded down with grocery bags. His mouth hung open and his hand still gripped the doorknob. She giggled, bumping the door closed with her hip and knocking him out of his reverie at the same time.

"So, where's your kitchen?"

She looked around the tiled entryway. A chandelier, dripping with crystals, took center stage. To the left and right of the door were small marble tables, each holding an expensive looking porcelain vase. *Those wouldn't last a day in my house*, was her first thought. Half her modest little cottage could fit in Dean's foyer. And looking up the wide, gleaming mahogany staircase, she knew there was a whole lot more house than this.

"Let me take some of those." Dean's gaze was bemused as he slipped a few of the bags out of Shannon's hands and nodded his head down a hall toward the back of what was clearly too big to have been given the title of summer home.

She followed quickly, trying to sneak a peek in each room that they passed. Oh, a pool table! Wow, an honest to goodness library, with a ladder attached to reach the higher shelves. Ms. Sheffield didn't have a library in the main house.

Shannon's grin widened when they reached the kitchen. Now this place definitely wasn't built for a bachelor who lived on dry cereal and peanut butter sandwiches. This kitchen was meant to host grand parties and state dinners. Shoving the bags on the nearest counter, Shannon turned a slow circle, taking in the stainless steel appliances, the yards of granite countertops. Everything was state of the art. And to think that it had all just been sitting here, unused, for all this time. It was a shame that such a bountiful kitchen should be so completely devoid of lingering cooking scents. Her imagination conjured a sweet, yeasty bread baking, and the pungent aroma of root veggies and beef simmering in a rich stock. Oh, the things she could create in here!

"So … I'm not sure what to say. I mean, 'thank you' is definitely in order, but …" Dean put his own bags down and began rustling through the contents.

"You rushed out of the store so fast that I figured you weren't nearly done with your shopping. I'm so sorry if we made you uncomfortable in there." Shannon got busy unpacking the reusable grocery bags.

"I hope you don't think I'm being pushy here, but I got a look in your cart before you took off." Shannon stuffed all the empties into one bag and pushed it to the center of the counter. "You don't really cook, do you, Dean?"

"That would be an understatement." He rubbed his stubble roughened chin, looking sheepish. "I haven't had to cook for myself. I guess when most guys are learning from their mothers, I was … busy." He stared at a point just over her left shoulder.

"Well, today is your lucky day, my friend. I am going to teach you to cook."

"And where is your posse while you are undertaking this thankless task?"

"I told you, it's your lucky day." She swatted him lightly on the arm. "The trips are in the process of being thoroughly run ragged so that by the time I pick them up they will beg for dinner and an early bedtime."

"I guess that makes it your lucky day, as well, then." His voice was a deep rumble she could feel inside her chest.

Dean leaned in close. He reached out a hand, his face so close she could feel his breath tickle her ear. Shannon caught just a hint of aftershave and her eyes nearly rolled back in her head. Oh, he smelled good! Without realizing it, she leaned in closer, her tongue darting out to wet her lips. Her eyes were focused on Dean's neck, the scent of his aftershave tempting her to see if he tasted as good as he smelled. Belatedly, she realized that his hand hadn't been reaching for her, but behind her, where he picked up a package of chicken and carried it to the fridge.

Shannon tried not to sound like a drowning person when she finally sucked in a couple lungfuls of air. She took the opportunity to compose her features once Dean's back was turned. Her heart was ricocheting all the way up and down her windpipe. She wiped damp palms on her jeans. Good lord, she had thought he was going to kiss her! Worse, she had wanted him to, and had felt a keening moment of regret when she realized she'd misread the situation.

"Are there any other perishables?" Dean had turned his attention back to her.

Not knowing if her voice would come out sounding wonky or not, Shannon decided not to chance speaking. Quickly, she scanned the items spread on the counter and slid the carton of eggs in his direction. She gathered up the frozen loaf of garlic bread and held it out at arm's length.

She shouldn't be here. This was a big mistake. No, leaving the kids with Talia was the bigger mistake. There would have been no chance for her out-of-work libido to suddenly get busy with three little munchkins watching every move they made. Shannon rubbed her bare arms, her skin suddenly prickly, too sensitive.

Dean was taking a long time putting things away. Shannon wondered if he was hiding in the fridge. Maybe she made him nervous. But he was in his own home now. He should be comfortable, right? How did this agoraphobia thing work?

Should she offer to leave? Who knew when she'd have another chance to help him help himself ... without having to run herd on her young crew? She shifted her weight from one foot to the other, worrying her bottom lip between her teeth. When was he finally going to turn around? *I've made a recluse even worse. I've broken him.* Tears pricked at the tender flesh of her eyelids.

"So what are we going to make first?"

Dean had shut the refrigerator and was now looking from Shannon to the rest of the groceries laid out on the counter. He didn't look freaked out. His smile was warm, friendly. His vibrant green eyes were a much darker shade than she remembered. Did he pay for those blonde highlights or were they natural? He coughed delicately. Oh God, he was waiting for an answer and Shannon was staring like a love-struck teen.

"I guess that would depend on what we have to work with." Shannon pasted a bright smile on her face and glanced around the spacious kitchen. "We've obviously got a stovetop and oven. The microwave will do in a pinch."

She almost apologized when she saw Dean wince at that last statement. She didn't intend to make him feel guilty for using one of modern science's greatest inventions. She just wanted him to know he had options, and those options grew exponentially when he thought outside of that stainless steel box.

"You mean, do I have pots and pans and all those doo-dads for cooking?" At her nod, he kept going. "Yeah, I think I'm about as well stocked as a person can get. They just don't get any use."

Shannon and Dean spent the next hour going through the kitchen. While they inventoried his cooking supplies, she quizzed him on what he liked to eat. His was a simple palate, classic meat and potatoes. He complained about the fact that there was no drive-thru burger joints within a fifteen-mile radius. Shannon actually had to agree with him on that one. Small towns, while charming, did have their drawbacks.

"There you go, that's all the more reason to learn to cook at home. It won't feel quite so much like a punishment."

"When we were on the road I'd get so sick of fast food, uh—" Dean cut himself off abruptly, and made a lot of noise clanging pots together underneath the counter.

He was hiding again. *On the road?* What did he mean by that? Shannon's brow wrinkled and she reached a finger up to smooth out the bunched skin. There was a lot more to her mysterious neighbor than she realized.

That may have been enough to turn away a lesser woman, but Shannon worked for a boss whom she saw maybe four months out of the year. Her days were consumed with cooking, cleaning, and keeping three preschoolers out of trouble. It wasn't enough to keep her imaginative brain active. She craved adventure, mystery. She could be way off base about Dean, but she was having too much fun trying to fill in the gaps. Now if she could only convince her body that her neighbor was off limits. Men were trouble; even men with tight buns who avoided potentially revealing conversation by practically climbing inside their kitchen cabinets.

CHAPTER FIVE

She must think I'm a horse's ass! Arms crossed over his bare chest as he raised his upper body off the floor for another crunch, Dean scowled. An image of the curvy redhead next door rose in his mind. He pictured her standing before him, delicate little hands braced on those scrumptious hips, a perfectly shaped brow lifted in mockery. *Avoid intimacy much?*

Dean closed his eyes and replayed the memory reel that had been on a loop since Shannon had left the other day. They'd been talking about not having the kids around. Naturally, his mind went … there. Who wouldn't want to take advantage of a little alone time with such a sexy woman? He'd almost kissed her! What had he been thinking? This self-imposed isolation was wreaking havoc on his control. And then slipping up by talking about his past?

He could have come clean. It would have been a hell of a lot easier than keeping his former identity secret. Dean was so tempted to trust that Shannon was not like all the others. But trust was earned, and he hadn't known Shannon long enough to build that platform.

Dean pumped out another set of sit-ups, then bounced up on the balls of his bare feet. He padded across the plush carpet and snagged his water bottle off the bedside table. Taking a few quenching gulps of liquid, he pushed open the slider and stepped out onto the balcony.

The balcony off the master suite of Dean's house (he refused to call it a mansion) was what had sold him on the place. The Atlantic Ocean, in all her glory, spread out before him. From here he could watch the whipped up froth of a nasty storm or the placid calm of a warm summer day. The salty tang in the air soothed his senses, reminded him of his place in Malibu. He closed his eyes and listened to the surf, imagining he was back home.

He settled into a wrought iron chair, put his water bottle on the mosaic-tiled bistro table, and reached for the guitar that was always close by. His fingers picked out chords on their own, his voice rumbling out words to a song he'd sung a thousand times, if not more. Did he miss his old life? Yeah, but not in the way he thought he would. Dean tapped his foot and bobbed his head in time to the song, staring absently at the unbroken surface of the water.

Shrieks of laughter reached his ears from a point just below him and to the left. Shannon's kids were playing in his yard again. He'd had to give up the ogre persona. They just weren't buying it. He grinned, thinking of the three little rapscallions from next door. They were exactly what he deserved for thinking he could just escape from the world and no one would notice.

Except it wasn't the kids who seemed to take the most notice. It was their mother. Shannon was so far removed from the type of women that ran in his social circle back home that he just didn't know what to think of her. *Is she for real?* Had crossed his mind on more than one occasion. She didn't seem to want anything from him. She thought she was helping him.

Okay, she was helping him. Dean didn't know a spatula from a saucepan and Shannon had nailed it when she suggested knowing a few cooking skills would increase his food choices. It had been second nature to pick up the phone, back in Malibu, for whatever tempted his palate. In Scallop Shores, however, the only thing he could get delivered was his mail. Learning to become more self-sufficient was definitely something Dean would benefit from. Getting to spend more time with his fiery neighbor wasn't too bad either.

Dean set the guitar down and stretched his long legs out on the chair opposite him. Reaching for his water bottle, he took a few pulls and wiped his mouth on his bare arm. He held the perspiring plastic bottle to his forehead and sighed as the coolness penetrated his heated skin. Eyes closed, he inhaled the clean scents around him. He picked out the beach roses that grew along the rocks. The tall pines were a sharp contrast. Then, ah, there it was. Shannon was putting her wet laundry out on the line. If he listened carefully, Dean could hear the snap of wet sheets and pillowcases.

He grinned. This woman had enough on her plate, raising three active five-year-olds. To bypass the convenience of a dryer spoke volumes about her character. Shannon was not afraid of hard work. In fact, Dean noticed she seemed to go out of her way to find the harder, more time-consuming way of doing something. Did the woman ever take a break? Did she have anyone who would help her out the way she had come to him?

Dean's cell phone suddenly chimed to life in the bedroom. He ran in and grabbed it off the bedside table, thumbing the answer button before bringing it to his ear.

"Dean, Marty Kincaid here. I'm just making sure you got that paperwork I sent over last week." *The paternity suit paperwork that wasn't worth the paper it was printed on? Yeah, got it.*

"I got the paperwork, Marty. It's a complete waste of both our time. You know that."

"So you want to settle this one? She's asking for a one-time payment of 2.4 million."

"2.4? Not two million or two and a half million? 2.4?" Dean snorted. "She's been watching too many lawyer shows on TV."

"How do you want to handle this one, Dean? Are we settling?"

Something in him snapped. This wasn't happening again. He refused to let this happen to him again. Nostrils flaring, fist clenching and unclenching, Dean gritted his teeth to keep from yelling at the lawyer who was really on his side.

"I'm not settling this one, Marty. I'm not the father. I know it. She knows it. She can rot in hell before she takes a free ride at my expense."

"But you usually just settle to avoid the drama. What if this draws you back into the spotlight?"

"Get a DNA test. Nail her to the wall with the results. That witch is not getting her hands on my money." Dean's mood was reflected in the white caps that had appeared on the ocean's surface. He glared at the horizon and the water got choppier still.

"I'm on it, buddy. We'll set an example by Ms. Cresswell. Maybe this will be the last woman who cries Daddy."

"She can be the last or not. I'm not letting myself be used as a convenient ATM ever again!" Dean disconnected the call and threw the phone on the bed.

The wind carried in the sound of the triplets giggling as they played. Dean was no longer in the mood to be charmed. Slamming the slider closed, he stalked from his bedroom. Pity party for one, now commencing.

• • •

"So, Brenna tells me your new neighbor is handsomer than her Ken doll. I'd say that's pretty high praise, coming from a five-year-old."

Shannon let out a belly laugh and clamped a hand over her mouth before she could wake the children sleeping down the hall. She snuggled into a corner of the couch, tucking her feet under a soft, yellow throw pillow. The laptop was perched on her knees and her mother smiled at her from 3,000 miles away.

"Yeah, Dean certainly has the 'Ken doll' look down. I can't wait until it gets a little warmer and we get to see him without his shirt on." She gasped in shock. "Oh God, I can't believe I just said that." Shannon darted her gaze away from the computer screen while a warm blush suffused her face and neck.

"Nothing wrong with that! Child, you closed yourself off to the opposite sex the second the door shut behind Vincent. You aren't a nun, Shannon. Women have needs too."

Fantastic. Modern technology has brought us Skype, so that we may now have intimately embarrassing conversations with our mothers on the other side of the country, face to face. Shannon frowned back at her mother. The amused grin on the older woman's face showed clearly that she didn't seem the least bit uncomfortable with the conversation.

"Look who's talking? Dad left when I was three. You never so much as looked at a man while I was growing up. You were always working."

"Not always. Like I said, women have needs too." Shannon's mom, Catherine, arched one perfectly waxed brow.

"Ew! Ew! So not going there!" Shannon waved her hands in front of her face, willing herself not to think of her mother sneaking out for late night bootie calls. She shuddered.

"Okay, I'm done lecturing. But it's clear you're interested in this guy. It would just be a shame if you wasted an opportunity because of your ... okay, *our* pasts." Catherine leaned in close and her face filled up most of the screen. "So tell me about Dean. The kids think he's the second coming."

"He's so nice, Mom. And he's great with the triplets. He can't tell Brady from Brian. I think he's too embarrassed to say anything though. I can tell Brenna is developing her first crush. She's already asked if she can have him over for a tea party ... and the rest of us are not invited."

Shannon reached out for her tea, cooling on the side table. She snagged a mini chocolate chip cookie from the small stack she'd allowed herself. Smiling at the computer screen, she nodded when Catherine lifted her own mug of tea and nibbled at a cookie that looked like it had come straight out of the same package Shannon's had.

They called this their weekly tea time. Catherine had Tuesday nights free. She would Skype with her grandchildren earlier in the evening, allowing Shannon time to clean up a little while her kids were busy talking. Then after Shannon put the triplets to bed, they reconnected for some mother/daughter time. Catherine kept Shannon supplied with various herbal teas that her friend Trudy sold in her shop in Carmel. Shannon, in turn, would send her mother packages of cookies that she'd loved while living in Maine but couldn't find in California.

"The poor guy." Shannon swallowed a bite of cookie and chased it with a quick sip of tea. "He's got agoraphobia." She shook her head sadly. "At least I think that's what's going on. He hides in his house every day, hardly ever comes out. When he's out in public, he's always looking over his shoulder. He just looks spooked, Mom."

Even alone in his house he didn't act 100% comfortable. He'd sure seemed out of sorts when she was there without the kids. Shannon had half expected him to climb all the way into the cupboards and pull the doors closed behind him. Maybe it was just her he was avoiding. Wow, that thought sucked.

"And if I know my girl, you have been trying to draw him out. You think he'd have a more full and satisfying life if he got out and lived a little. How am I doing?" Catherine snapped a cookie in half and popped one piece in her mouth.

"Yeah, only I've just been thinking that I'm probably pushing too hard. Maybe I'm the reason he seems so uncomfortable."

"Or maybe he's dealing with his own man/woman issues and doesn't know how to tell you he's attracted to you?"

"Geez, Mom, when did you get so romantic? It's like you're seeing couples everywhere."

"Funny you should say that."

43

Shannon's heart thumped double time and she had the crazy urge to slam the laptop shut, running from the room with her hands over her ears yelling "lalalala." Schooling her features so she didn't look as freaked out as she felt, Shannon took a deep breath.

"What's going on, Mom?"

"I'm bringing someone with me when I visit next month. Someone special." Now it was Catherine's turn to blush; the gentle pink made her eyes sparkle brighter. She looked ten years younger.

"I don't know if there's room. Ms. Sheffield will be here with a houseful of guests." Shannon bit her lip, hoping her excuse was enough for her mother to abandon the idea of bringing her man friend.

"Oh, don't worry about putting us up, dear. We're planning on staying at the Rose Arbor, that old bed and breakfast on Route 1."

"But you always stay with us!" Shannon's tone was wheedling, but she didn't care. "What will I tell the kids?"

"Oh, for heaven's sake, Shannon, I'll be ten minutes down the road. It won't change our visit in the least," Catherine tsked.

"I'm sorry. I don't know why I said that." Shannon held on to a brittle smile for all she was worth. "Of course we'll have a great time. The kids can't wait to see you again."

By silent agreement, the women moved on to safer topics: Catherine's job at the art gallery, the beautiful weather in Carmel, the pesto pizza Shannon made for dinner that night. They finished their tea and cookies. Catherine shook her nearly-empty box and remarked that she'd have to make room in her luggage for as many boxes as she could fit. Gently, she touched the screen, as though she could feel her daughter's soft cheek beneath her fingertips.

"It's getting late for you, sweetheart. I'm going to sign off and let you get some rest."

"I love you, Mom. Talk to you next week." They waved and blew kisses as they reached out to shut down their Skype sessions.

Shannon sighed as she carried the laptop to the dining room table. She returned for her tea mug, breathing deeply of the lingering scents of chamomile and spearmint. Dropping the mug and the plate of cookie crumbs in the sink, Shannon brushed off her hands on a dishtowel. Her fingers itched to go back and wash and dry those two items sitting in the sink. Shaking her head, she snapped off the overhead light and darted out of the kitchen before she could go back and work ... again. "You're off duty," she reminded herself.

Tip-toeing down the hall, though her triplets probably could have slept through an earthquake, Shannon peeked into Brenna's room. The little girl had kicked off her covers and was currently facing the footboard. Shannon tucked the comforter around her, making sure Gabriella Tink, Brenna's current favorite teddy bear, was within reach.

In Brian and Brady's room, Shannon had to navigate her way through a minefield of tiny cars and trucks in order to reach the beds. She gathered a stack of picture books from Brady's bed and returned them to the basket on the floor. She kissed his temple, smoothing a lock of hair down that would surely spring back to life by morning. Brian lay on his tummy, his little behind sticking up in the air, just like he'd slept since he was a baby. Shannon dropped a kiss on his velvety cheek as she pulled the blankets up for him. With a last, lingering look, Shannon left the boys' bedroom. Oh, these kids were her life. She would do anything in the world for them.

Slipping into a comfy pair of pink fleece pajamas, Shannon slid between the cool sheets of her big bed. Her oversized bed. She stretched out, spread eagle, and still didn't come near the edges of the bed. She rolled over and snuggled into the pillows. Who would have thought her mother would be the one to suggest she tend to her "woman's needs"? Ugh. Now the idea had been planted, Shannon couldn't stop squirming.

She pictured the mattress sinking as a warm body climbed in and spooned her from behind. No surprise whom that warm body belonged to. She could almost hear Dean's deep voice rumbling in her ear. She flopped over, the emptiness of the other side of the bed making it appear twice as big. Shutting her eyes against the depressing sight, Shannon ignored the single tear that managed to sneak past her defenses and slide down her cheek.

CHAPTER SIX

The morning had turned quickly, from balmy to sticky. Dean stripped off his t-shirt, using it to mop his forehead before tossing it to the ground. In Malibu he'd hired workers to mow his lawn, trim the edges, and keep his yard looking neat. Perhaps there were yard maintenance workers out here in Maine, too, but the fewer people trampling through his property the better. Scowling, Dean remembered the times he'd found reporters and photographers camped out in his bushes. The mile-high security gates hadn't been an obstacle—and neither had their morals, apparently.

So he'd mowed his own lawn. It'd been a hell of a lot bigger than he had realized. And he had learned the hard way that his lawn mower didn't come with the handy feature that collects the clippings. And so he had raked. Contemplating a visit to the nearest home improvement warehouse for the latest in time-saving lawn maintenance equipment, Dean attacked the weeds growing under the rose bushes.

Sitting back on his haunches, he surveyed the yard. Not bad for a first timer. His head guy in Malibu, Luis, would have cut the grass on the diagonal. He left nice, neat rows. Dean's yard on this opposite coast had long, wobbly lines that looked mostly like he'd taken nearly as many beer breaks as he had lawn-cutting time. Practice. That's all he needed.

A rustling sounded where he now knew the break in the hedge to be. Dean caught a flash of bright blue and an even brighter shade of brilliant copper. Shannon must have turned her back, for her little chicks were flying the coop. His upper lip curling in amusement, Dean turned his own back. They played this game nearly every day now. The triplets snuck into his yard and he pretended not to notice. Intensely curious, they followed him about, hiding wherever they could find cover. At some point, Shannon would call for the children and they would run scampering home.

Brushing his palms against well-worn denim, Dean strode off toward the shed. He had bought several flats of flowers, intending to brighten up the yard, make it seem more like home. The patter of little sneakers sounded behind him. Giving them enough time to duck out of sight, Dean turned with exaggerated slowness. He chuckled when he spied one of the boys scrunched down behind the lawnmower. Brenna posed, stiff as a statue, behind a skinny sapling. He couldn't see the other one, but knew they traveled in threes.

"Boy, there sure are a lot of flowers to plant. I may have gotten in over my head here. I wish I had some help."

As he'd predicted, the kids burst from their hiding places, eager smiles glued to their tiny faces. Everyone chattered at once. Brenna complimented him on his choice of colors. Brian offered suggestions on what tools they would need. Brady gestured, with huge sweeps of his arms, where he thought the flowers would look best. Dean shoved a hand through his hair, looking from one child to another and trying desperately to keep track of the conversation. What had he gotten himself into?

Taking the lead, before it could be taken from him, Dean hefted a bag of gardening soil to the maple tree at the back of the lawn. He ringed the tree with some healthy nutrients and then returned for some bright yellow marigolds. His little helpers dove right in, obviously no strangers to planting spring flowers. Dean looked at the brand new gardening gloves he'd left sitting with the rest of the supplies, tags still attached. Then he looked down at the triplets. They were elbow-deep in soil and dirt from around the tree. Each one of them had a smudge somewhere on their face.

Shrugging aside any reservations, Dean dropped to his knees, summoned his inner child, and dug his bare hands into the soil.

Oh, it felt good. Digging the ground brought back memories he hadn't thought about in years. Dean and his brother, Flynn, used to dig in the backyard for hours. One day, they would be searching for long-lost treasure. Another day, they could be burying something infinitely valuable. He grinned and swiped at his jaw, recalling the time they swore they had discovered a dinosaur. It turned out to be a beloved pet from some previous owner of their house. The morbidity of stumbling upon a grave had thrilled the young boys to no end.

Working alongside his pint-sized neighbors, Dean actually found himself having a good time. He'd never spent much time around young children. He assumed they always needed their noses wiped, whined at the tiniest thing, and needed help with absolutely everything. Color him surprised when the triplets were the ones to explain to him roughly how far apart to plant the marigold starts. Dean nearly ripped the first one in half as he struggled to pull it out of the plastic container. Brady laid a gentle hand on his arm and showed him how to tap the bottom of the pot to jiggle the plant loose.

Remembering something from the other day, Dean tried his hand at conversation.

"So, Brenna, how is Rosie doing?" He held his breath as he waited to see if this was a tear-inducing topic or if it was relatively safe.

She giggled and shook her head slowly, as if he were the small child and she the wise, mature adult. "She's right here. Why don't you ask her yourself?"

Uh oh. The pressure was on, too, as the boys had turned to see how Dean would handle this situation. Brian looked quite smug, clearly expecting him to fall on his face. Brady looked like he felt sorry for him, his own smile a little sad. Taking a deep breath and facing this challenge he'd brought on himself, Dean turned to face the empty space beside Brenna. *Okay, it's go time.*

"Hello there, Rosie. How are you on this fine sunshiny day?"

"Mr. Dean? Rosie is watching us from the tree branch." Brenna pointed right above his head. She wasn't going to make this easy on him at all.

Expecting the boys to have a good laugh at his expense, Dean jumped when the laughter he heard came in melodic peals from behind him. He sprang to his feet, turning around and wiping his grimy hands on his jeans. He waited for a good ribbing from Shannon but it turned out he wasn't the only one caught by surprise. She had stopped laughing and now stood staring, with her mouth forming an O.

"Um, hi. I found these trespassers and decided to use them for slave labor as punishment. Though Rosie, there, just isn't pulling her weight."

He had meant it to be funny, but caught the wince that pinched Shannon's features for the briefest of moments. Her hands were on her hips and she looked tired. Her smiling cherubs, fortunately, didn't notice the tension and continued to look as innocent as they surely felt.

"Hey, let's try and remove a layer or two of this dirt and I'll go get us a drink."

Dean ushered the kids to the side of the house where the hose was kept reeled. Shannon ran ahead, let out a length of hose and turned on the water. She ordered all hands turned out for a spray down, including him in the lineup. She aimed the hose at Brenna's dirty toes, peeking out of their sequined sandals. The boys howled in mock horror as their mother pretended to lose control of the hose and soaked them down good.

"Please, don't shoot!" Dean held up his hands in surrender, waiting to be Shannon's next target. Even minus one shirt, it was a hot afternoon and the spray would definitely be welcome.

Looking up at him through thick lashes, he caught a hint of pure feminine lust, before she swallowed hard and ducked her head. Instead of turning the hose on him, she handed Dean the nozzle and backed away. Apparently, playtime was over.

Muttering something about going in for some juice, Dean beat a hasty retreat for the kitchen. He refused to acknowledge the feeling of not being included in the playful repartee as disappointment. He wasn't part of their family. It shouldn't matter. He was living the solitary life. Sometimes the solitary life sucked.

• • •

Shannon stuffed her hands in her pockets and stared hungrily as Dean strode past her. His broad back glistened with sweat. Blond hair curled damply against his neck. Two dirty handprints, one on each cheek, decorated his tight jeans. Large handprints they were, too. The man had some seriously good genes.

Taking a deep breath, Shannon turned to face her children. She couldn't yell at them for sneaking over here. She'd known darned well what they were up to. She had all but given the go ahead when she turned her focus to weeding out her vegetable garden. And it wasn't just today. Yesterday, she had watched them sidle through the hedge while she was busy clipping coupons at the patio table. The day before, it had been while she was washing the windows.

If the triplets just happened to end up in Dean's yard, then gosh darned it, it would be remiss of her not to go over and retrieve them. God, when had she turned into such a sex-starved stalker? She had to put a stop to this now.

"Hey, guys, we've talked about this. It might have been okay to come over and play in this yard when no one lived here. But the rules have changed now. Mr. Dean lives here and he deserves his privacy."

"But we were helpin' him, Mommy." Brenna's eyes were huge, her expression sincere.

"Yeah, he said he bought too much flowers and didn't know what he was gonna do," Brady added.

"And that was Mr. Dean's very polite way of making the best out of a frustrating situation." The kids just stared blankly.

"Actually, we were having fun. Really." Dean had slipped up behind them. He gestured for the kids to head on up to the big cedar deck. Placing one of those magnificently large hands at the small of Shannon's back and guided her up the steps.

"Uh, so I figured beer was out. I'm not sure what the younger crowds are drinking these days, so I poured them some orange juice. I hope that's okay."

Still getting over the shock of Dean touching her, instead of running for cover, Shannon could only nod. Her children were tearing through a bag of double-stuff Oreos. She made a mental note to buy him a replacement. She lowered herself into a patio chair and accepted the icy cold Corona that Dean handed her.

"We aren't kids, right?" He winked.

Shannon returned his warm smile, while resisting the urge to crawl into his lap. Dear God, would the man please put on a shirt! Her poor, deprived (or was it depraved) body couldn't take the torture. *Breathe, Shannon. He's just a man.* And she was not in the market for one of those. But as long as he was going to sit in front of her, half-naked, she'd enjoy the show. She wasn't a nun.

"This isn't what you wanted, what you expected, when you moved up here. I'm sorry for that."

"I'm learning to be flexible."

"Yes, but you shouldn't have to." Shannon took a fortifying sip of beer and set the sweating bottle back on the table. "I promised to keep them out of your yard and I've broken my promise."

"I'm not complaining, Shannon. Have you heard me tell them to get out?" The words came out in a deep rumble that sent shivers up her spine.

"What can I say? You are very kind."

"Oh, just stuff it!" Shannon's raised eyebrows reached her hairline. "Yeah, I was trying to hide at first. I'm still trying to hide." Dean rubbed a thumb back and forth over the gold and blue Corona label. "But not from you guys."

"You said you wanted peace and quiet. You wanted us to give you your space." She found herself mesmerized by the motion of that thumb, wishing it were her hand he was stroking, instead of a beer bottle.

"I may have been wrong." His bright green eyes focused on the glass bottle in front of him.

He looked nervous. Was he making a play? Oh, God! Did she even want him to? Shannon leaned forward in her chair, twisting her head to the side so he was forced to meet her gaze. They just sat, quietly studying each other. That thumb had stopped rubbing. Dean dropped his hand to the glass tabletop. Boldly, Shannon covered it with hers. She had expected him to yank his away and was happy to be mistaken.

Smiling shyly, Shannon sat back in her chair and raised her face to the sun. The heat warmed her limbs, made her want to curl up like a cat and take a nap. She hadn't felt this relaxed in so long. A shrill scream rent the air, turning her blood to ice. Shannon whipped her head around. The triplets had abandoned their snack and juice and were no longer on the deck. Scrambling out of her chair, she saw Dean streaking across the lawn.

"Mommy! Brady's hurt, Brady's hurt," Brenna choked out in breathless sobs.

Shannon raced to her son, fear giving her feet wings. Dean already cradled the injured boy in his lap, beneath the maple tree. Brian and Brenna made room for their mother to sink to the ground in front of Dean. Her assessing gaze studied her son, starting at his mussed hair and traveling down his body. When she got to his chest and saw him holding his left arm tight to his body with his right, she blew out a long breath and tried to put on a smile for Brady's benefit.

"Aw, baby. Can you lift your arm?" They all waited, breath held, as Brady attempted to raise his arm, and failed.

"I'm sorry, I'm so sorry." Brady was crying and when Shannon tried to take him from Dean, he held on tight. "I'm so very sorry." She realized Brady was trying to apologize to Dean.

"What's to be sorry about, bud? I should be apologizing to you, leaving that dangerous tree here." Dean's attempt at humor earned a small, watery smile.

"Your flowers. I busted up your flowers." Everyone looked down to see that roughly half the flowers they had planted were now trampled flat.

"Hey, if those flowers helped cushion your fall and kept you from breaking *both* arms, then it was well worth it."

Shannon walked quickly beside Dean as he carried Brady up to the house. She silently cursed herself for being the worst mother ever. Way to pay attention! Her kid was off climbing trees, unbeknownst to her because she had been busy making goo-goo eyes at the neighbor.

How could she have been so selfish? The first time she let her guard down and one of her babies got hurt. Shannon swallowed back the sob that burned in her lungs. There would be time for crying later.

CHAPTER SEVEN

They were lucky it wasn't a compound fracture. Dean had seen someone fall off the stage during rehearsal once, and the resulting break had shoved the ankle bone out of the skin like it was a jagged knife. He didn't mind admitting he had come damned close to throwing up when he saw it. Brady was trying so hard not to cry. The poor guy was putting on such a brave front. Probably didn't want to scare his mom any more than he had. Dean totally got that.

"We can take my SUV. There is plenty of room for the kids in the back." Dean strode purposefully toward the driveway.

"They need their booster seats. I've got this, Dean. It's not your responsibility." She was shutting him out. Her eyes reflected the cold steel that had slammed down between them.

"Fine. You take Brady to the emergency room and I'll watch the other two."

Still carrying the little boy, Dean hurried to Shannon's yard and waited at the blue minivan for her to run in and grab her purse and the car keys. Brenna sniffled quietly at his side. Shannon hurried back to the car and opened the door. Gently, Dean deposited Brady in the nearest car seat and was nudged aside before he could even reach for the seat belt.

"He's my son. I'll buckle him in." Mama bear was showing her claws. "Brian, Brenna, get in the car."

"Shannon, this is ridiculous. You need to focus on Brady. You can't do that with the other two there."

"Do *not* tell me what to do. I have this under control. I do not need your help." Her fingers trembled as she fastened the seat belt.

Dean waited until she was done and gently drew her aside. Shannon refused to meet his eyes. He rubbed his hands up and down her arms, trying to sooth rattled nerves, trying to shore up her strength. He remained silent. If he tried to hold her she might come undone, and she wouldn't want the kids to see her like that. Holding her at arm's length, Dean watched Shannon as she silently waged an inner battle.

"You need to be the best mom you can be to Brady right now. Let me watch Brian and Brenna. Please. It's the only way I can think of to start making this up to you."

Shannon's head snapped up and she stared at him in confusion. "You didn't do anything. This isn't your fault. I wasn't watching him. It's my job to protect him." Hysteria edged the words that had Dean's heart squeezing painfully.

He continued to rub her arms and waited for the hitch in her breathing to go back to normal. Her eyes never left his face. It wasn't that she didn't trust him with her children. He understood that. It was the damned responsibility she couldn't seem to relinquish. Shannon was determined to do it all on her own. She swallowed hard and tugged her arms out of his grasp, wrapping them tightly around her middle.

"Don't feed them a ton of sugar if you don't want to deal with a couple of crazy animals. I'll be back as soon as I can." She tore her gaze away and herded up the other two children. "Be good for Mr. Dean. Cut him some slack, huh? Brady and I will be back soon. I bet he'll have a super cool cast for you two to sign." Hooking an arm around each child, she hugged them hard and dropped a kiss on both carrot-topped heads.

Dean gathered the kids out of the way of the minivan and waved goodbye. Everyone stood awkwardly for a few moments. As the reality of the situation hit, he was stunned to realize he'd just offered to watch not one, but two five-year-olds. He'd never babysat a day in his life! Were they potty trained? *Please, God, let them be potty trained.*

"Let's plant more flowers. We can fix the squished parts," Brian declared.

"Yeah, that will make Brady feel better." Brenna slipped her hand into Dean's as they headed back to his yard by way of the break in the Arborvitae.

Simple logic, really, but it worked for him. Dean and the remaining two triplets cleared the ruined marigolds away and planted more. He really had bought more than he had any idea what to do with. Brenna and Brian hauled a heavy watering can to the tree and Dean helped them lift it to sprinkle the ring of newly planted flowers with water. Then, once again, they headed for the hose to rinse their messy hands and knees.

Panic tried to rear its head again, now that a new activity did not immediately present itself. *What would Shannon do?* Dean thought to himself. He remembered her warning about sugary snacks and thought it best to stay away from food altogether.

"Can we watch TV?" Brenna batted her eyelashes hopefully.

"Yeah, got any movies?"

Dean mentally went through the stack of DVDs he owned, trying to rate them in terms of suitability. Most were of the "blow 'em up" variety. Shannon would have his head. He didn't think he owned anything Disney-esque. Eh, they could find something On Demand.

Not fully comfortable with two five-year-olds parking it on his couch for an extended length of time, Dean suggested they both use the bathroom. He raised a silent prayer that they wouldn't need his help in there.

The gods were smiling down at him this time. He didn't have to wipe any butts. If it stayed this easy, he could actually handle this babysitting thing.

"Mr. Dean, can I sit in your lap?" Brenna sat on the couch, looking tiny and very vulnerable.

Dean looked from her to her brother. They waited, expectantly. He hadn't actually intended to watch the movie with them. He had a lot of email to catch up on. Already seated in his comfy recliner, laptop open and booting up, Dean hoped they would take the hint. Nope.

Oh, wow, this was *so* out of his comfort zone. Dean settled on the couch and waited for Brenna to climb onto his lap. She curled a strand of hair around her forefinger and snuggled into his chest.

Apparently assuming that this was a party, and anyone could join in, Brian shifted across the cushions until he was flattened against Dean's side. With his one remaining free hand, Dean flipped through the offerings on the screen. The kids ended up choosing *Charlotte's Web*, assuring him they had this at home and watched it all the time.

"Mr. Dean? Do you think Brady is okay?"

"I think he's probably feeling much better now that he's gotten a lot of fussing over by all the doctors and nurses at the ER."

He knew a lot had ridden on that answer, as he could feel both tiny bodies melt with relief. Poor kids were scared for their brother. Dean bet they'd never had to be split up like this before. He placed a comforting arm around each child and settled in to watch a barnyard full of animals talk like humans.

● ● ●

She owed him big. It had been a few days since Shannon had collected the kids from Dean's house and rushed off. She hadn't known what to say then, and she didn't have a clearer idea now. Shannon watched the kids running through the sprinkler, Brady's cast wrapped in a plastic bag to keep it dry. She was hovering, she knew it, keeping her precious family in a bubble. She was so used to going it alone that her instincts told her to shut out the world.

Dean had stopped by the day after the accident. He knocked at the door, standing on the porch with the biggest teddy bear she had ever seen. It would have been so easy to open the door, let him into their bubble. But she didn't. Seeing him brought all that guilt to the forefront. She recalled reaching for Dean's hand on his deck, then hearing Brady scream. Bile clawed at her throat as she ignored the rapping. Tears pricked her eyelids when the triplets asked why she wouldn't let Mr. Dean in.

Now who was playing the hermit? Shannon slouched in her lawn chair, her eyes drawn to the gap in the arborvitae. *Come back over*, she willed. *No, don't!* Oh, this was insane. She had proven that hormones clouded her mothering instincts. Compartmentalize. She could do this. Shove all that lust into a deep dark box, wrap it in chains, and throw a big ol' boulder on it for good measure.

A high shriek had Shannon halfway out of her chair before she realized it was a shriek of delight. She stood up, rubbing her arms briskly. She flashed an overly bright smile at the triplets so they wouldn't be alarmed. Brady waved his grocery bag-wrapped arm at her. Bless him, he was such a trooper. She was so lucky to have her children. They were her life. She didn't need anything ... or anyone else.

"Great day for a run in the sprinkler, isn't it?"

Shannon's head snapped around and she jumped back to find Dean standing right behind her.

"So, yeah, I can see the attraction. Sneaking through that hedge is kind of fun." His bright eyes were full of merriment.

"I believe our roles have officially reversed." She knew she was sounding snotty, but if it pushed him away, so much the better.

"Are you asking me to leave?" His quiet voice sounded just the tiniest bit hurt.

He'd given her an out. Shannon closed her eyes, blew out a sigh, and pictured that box. Mentally, she tugged on the chains and hoped to God they'd hold. She opened her eyes and gave him a half smile.

"I want to apologize. I didn't thank you properly for saving my butt the other day. You did me a huge favor, watching Brian and Brenna for me."

"It's what neighbors do. We help each other."

"Neighbors." The chains on that box started rattling and she added a huge troll to sit atop the boulder. There. She could do this.

"So, how's the patient?" Dean paused and did a double-take when he saw the plastic bag encasing Brady's plaster cast.

"Couldn't ask for a better one. He's been so cheerful, doesn't complain. Loves the attention, naturally. As long as he has regular doses of ice cream, he's a champ."

"And how is his mom? I've got to admit, she didn't look so good when I saw her last."

"His mom is up to her eyeballs in mommy-guilt right now. But she'll pull through. Just give her a little time." Shannon lifted her shoulders to her ears and let them drop back down.

"It's a rite of passage, you know? Every kid has to have that cool story that they can talk up at camp or sleepovers or whatever."

"Oh, yeah? What was your rite of passage?" Shannon looked Dean up and down, trying to figure out where his battle scars lay.

"Mine? I was riding on the back of my buddy's bike—barefoot. Foot slipped, got mangled in the spokes. Took most of the skin off the top. Wasted too much of the summer on the couch. I would have much rather broken my arm."

Shannon's face scrunched up in disgust and her muscles bunched in commiseration. Just hearing that one made her hurt. She caught herself as her hand had already begun to reach out, to comfort the child that Dean had been. *Stop it!*

Ironically, it was Dean who reached out to sooth. He clasped Shannon's hand in his own and squeezed, holding it just a moment before letting it go.

"Just don't wallow too long, okay? You really have nothing to feel guilty about."

He dashed over to the kids, pretending that the spray of water was a force field he couldn't penetrate. They howled with laughter. Shannon tried not to notice how perfect they all looked together.

CHAPTER EIGHT

Dean nearly fell from bed in his haste to answer the doorbell. It wasn't even 8 o'clock in the morning. Something had to be wrong at Shannon's. He stubbed his toe on the bedroom doorframe and slid down the first three stairs. His heart knocked at his chest as loudly as the banging on the door. Who was hurt this time?

"Dino! 'Bout damned time. Did I wake you?" The chuckle that followed suggested his dear friend, and former bandmate, was quite pleased with himself.

"Jax? What the hell are you doing here?"

Dean dug the heels of his hands into his eyes and blew out a noisy sigh of frustration. The fear Dean had felt upon waking had pulled his nerves taut. Now, as they relaxed, he was left totally wrung out.

"Dude, you went off the radar. Everyone's asking about you."

He didn't even bother to hide the snort that particular news elicited. Leading the way into the kitchen at the back of the house, Dean gestured to a stool at the granite counter. He filled the carafe with water and played thumb war with the coffee filters. Knowing Jax didn't like his coffee strong, Dean threw an extra scoop into the basket, his humor somewhat restored.

"So ... what? You take the red eye in?"

"Surprise." Jax leaned in and snagged an apple out of the wire basket in the center of the island. He took a huge bite and grinned around the mouthful.

"I told you guys I wanted some time. We'll have the house warming to end all house warmings, but ..." He pinched the bridge of his nose.

The coffee finished brewing and Dean doctored his, leaving Jax to fend for himself. He stepped out onto the deck and stood at the railing. His eyes were drawn to the patio table, where he and Shannon had begun to have a "moment."

Then, because she felt that her son's fall from the tree was actually her fault, she had erected this ridiculous wall. Even crazier was the fact that this frustrated and disappointed him to no end. He was supposed to be hiding out from all things female. Women were trouble. Women were paternity suits and settlements, headaches and ... And yet, Shannon was none of that.

"Whatcha thinkin' about?" Jax leaned a hip against the rail and grimaced as he took a slug of coffee.

"How complicated life can be." Dean closed his eyes and breathed deep, the now familiar scents of the Atlantic coastline a soothing balm.

"What's her name?"

"Shannon. Hey!" He glared over the rim of his coffee mug.

"You came here to get away from the estrogen set and things got even more messed up, huh?"

"In a nutshell."

Jax swirled the liquid around in his cup, his grin having finally disappeared. He stared intently at the tree line. Dean groaned inwardly. Oh, he knew that look. He was being ambushed. Well, it didn't matter. His answer was no.

"Out with it." Dean wheeled on his friend and pinned him with a pointed look.

"This reality show contacted Jordie. They want to get the whole band in for interviews. Do some 'where are they now?' type stuff, ya know?"

"Have fun with that. I'll pass." He flung the dregs of his mug over the railing. Whether to fertilize or kill the lawn below, time would tell.

"It just means a quick trip back, Dino. Then you and Shannon can unravel whatever is making things complicated." Jax sat down in a patio chair, stretching out his long legs.

"Ha!" Dean's laugh was curt. "Stop calling me Dino. It's Dean now. It's been Dean for a long time now. I'm done with that life. It was fun while it lasted, but I'm done." He started pacing, frowning when he tried to shove his hands into his jeans pockets, only to remember he was wearing sweats. "And this thing with Shannon? It's being 'Dino' that is making it complicated!"

"Is she star-struck? After your millions? Has she asked you to introduce her to anyone yet?" Jax was every bit as familiar with the downside of dating when you were a celebrity as Dean was.

"She doesn't know," he spoke very softly.

"She doesn't know how much you're worth?" Jax stood up and stalked closer, a hand on his shoulder stopping Dean from wearing a path on the cedar planks.

"Shannon doesn't know I'm Dino Valentine. She doesn't know I used to be in a boy band. She doesn't know she's living next door to a celebrity has-been, or that I'm running away from yet another fake paternity suit." That's what was complicated.

• • •

The sun had already pushed its way through the early morning fog. The day was shaping up to be a hot one. Shannon finished wiping down the kitchen counters and tossed the sponge into the sink. Her little slug-a-beds had only just stumbled out for some Cheerios and juice. The usual morning chatter was replaced by yawns and bored sighs. Everyone picked listlessly at their breakfast. Time to shake things up a bit.

"Supposed to be a hot one today." This was met with groans. "It would probably be a little cooler by the shore." *Wait for it...*

"Yeah! We're going to the beach!" Brian scrambled from his chair, sloshing milk on the table in his hurry to take his cereal bowl to the sink.

"Can we invite Drake and Danny to come with us? I still haven't showed them my cast." Brady visibly vibrated with excitement.

"Let's see if they have any plans for today. Tumble Tots is closed."

The kids raced off to put on swim trunks and a bathing suit. Shannon called her friend to invite her and the twins to the beach. Between Memorial Weekend and Labor Day Weekend, parking anywhere near the beach was challenging, to say the least. The early bird got the parking spot, and woe betide anyone forgetting to pack quarters. Oh, how the town relied on tourist season!

Leaving the triplets to figure out what sand toys, floats, and other essential toys to bring to the beach, Shannon packed a cooler. Ah, the first beach day of the season. She reached for the peanut butter but then remembered that little Danny was allergic to peanuts. Knowing her children's penchant for sharing, that wasn't a chance she was willing to take. Jam sandwiches it would be, then.

Shannon quickly sliced up a bunch of strawberries and slipped them in a baggie, looking forward to later in the summer when the blueberries would be ripe. She snagged a package of goldfish crackers out of the pantry, deciding to bring the whole bag, just to be on the safe side. She had already retrieved the beach cooler from the garage of the big house, hoping a great day would present itself soon.

She carried the heavy cooler, loaded down with food, drinks, and all the ice packs she could fit. Brenna stumbled out of the house in her Hello Kitty one-piece, swim goggles covering her eyes and a bright pink swim ring around her waist. Brian and Brady, using his one good arm, dragged a huge LL Bean tote bag full of every shovel, pail and sand mold they owned. Shannon suspected that, were she to look, the backyard sandbox would be completely devoid of toys.

Everyone scrambled up into their booster seats while Shannon loaded their beach-going supplies in the back of the minivan. Before she closed the trunk, she stopped and listened. There was the excited noise—the chatter and the giggling that had been missing this morning. She paused and looked over at the house next door.

Strange, but she almost felt guilty not asking Dean along. He'd probably say no, anyway. He didn't seem to mind spending time with her little brood in the safety of their two houses, but the guy still wigged out over going into town. Shrugging, she hopped in the van and hoped the parking space gods were looking out for her.

The public lot was full, not a big surprise. Shannon drove through the meandering one-way street that looped around one of the three major beach areas. It wasn't the closest to home, but with a zoo, amusement park, shops, and restaurants lining every square inch of space, it was definitely the most fun. She found a lone parking spot in a small lot that belonged to a fruit stand. They had a ton of foot traffic, so they probably wouldn't begrudge her the space. Bonus points that she didn't have to plug a parking meter!

Shannon's monster cooler had wheels and a long, wide handle that could be collapsed when not in use. Those features sure came in handy now. She loaded all their beach-going supplies on the lid of the cooler. Taking the hand of the nearest triplet, she checked to make sure they were making their chain. As they'd gotten older, transporting these three had gotten much easier. Shannon no longer felt like she was trapped in her little cottage.

They met up with Talia and her boys on the boardwalk in front of the arcade. The kids were torn between wanting to rush right for the surf and wanting to play endless games of nickel skeeball. Shannon promised them a roll of nickels later in the afternoon. Satisfied, they jumped off the boardwalk and raced to find some rocks to anchor their beach blanket. Shannon and Talia followed, each loaded down with a day's worth of fun.

"How ya holding up?" Talia adjusted the brim of her large sunhat and leaned back against her beach chair.

"I'm fine. What are you talking about?" Absently, she dug in the wet sand at her feet with a stick.

"I know you, Shan. And we aren't that different. Brady got hurt on your watch. You're bound to feel all kinds of guilty right now. Spill."

Shannon shaded her eyes, watching a pleasure boat cruise by. She could barely make out the occupants, all of them young and scantily clad. Not a care in the world. They could flirt all they wanted. They could lose themselves in the moment, live life just for them.

"I forgot myself. I started to feel. I started to think I could have it all." She was speaking softly, shame squeezing her throat as she forced the words through.

"Oh, crap—you were having a moment!" Talia clamped her hands down on her chair and angled it to face Shannon more directly. "Now listen to me. The timing sucked. I'll give you that. But don't think for a second that Brady got hurt because you were getting to know your hottie neighbor."

"I'm not stupid. I know he would have climbed that tree regardless of whether he knew I was watching or not."

"But you're his mom and you can't resist beating yourself up about it."

"Bingo."

Shannon leaned out of her chair and snagged a bottle of water from the cooler. She ran the cold plastic across her overheated forehead before twisting the cap and taking a long drink. She focused on the castle taking shape a few feet away. All five kids were working as a team.

"Remember a few months ago, when Danny had to have five stitches in his chin? Jeff made me swear not to tell anyone the whole story ... but you need to hear this."

Shannon capped her water and gave Talia her full attention. Her friend took a deep breath, bright pink dotting her high cheekbones.

"It wasn't naptime for the boys yet. But Jeff was horny. So we put them in their room and told them to read books. We'd have a quickie and then go get them, right?"

Shaking her head in commiseration, Shannon grimaced. She remembered that incident ... well, the part she had been told about. Drake had opened his dresser drawers like stairs, climbed up and jumped from the top of the dresser. He landed on his brother, Danny, who fell against the corner of the toy chest. He'd split open his chin.

"It happens to all of us. There is no such thing as a perfect parent. We're all human." Talia covered Shannon's hand with one of her own. "Putting your own needs first is healthy. It's not selfish. Bottling them up until they're out of control? That's not good for anyone."

"Says the mother who had to take her son in for stitches because she was putting her needs first."

"Oh, you want to talk mommy guilt? That kid got a new toy every day for almost two weeks." Shannon laughed at that. Her heart felt lighter than it had since Brady's accident. She would get through this.

CHAPTER NINE

Dean shoved the brim of his baseball cap low over his eyes. His mirrored sunglasses completed his incognito look. He shot an exasperated look at Jax, who had taken the proffered hat but flipped it backward.

"Do you even care that I have spent the last couple of weeks keeping as low a profile as possible? If you're recognized, then it's only a matter of seconds before they realize that the idiot with you is part of the band."

"You say that like it's a bad thing. Lighten up, dude. You think we're gonna get mobbed?" The tone of his voice suggested Jax would rather enjoy the prospect.

"It's not just the people that live in Scallop Shores. This is a tourist town. There are a heck of a lot more people walking around here this time of year."

"Then A: You picked the wrong town to hide your butt in; and B: You picked the wrong time of year to settle in."

"Or C: I made a huge mistake giving you my address." Dean tipped his shades down and stared hard at his friend. Jax merely grinned.

Resigned to the fact that he was to play tour guide, Dean backed his SUV out of the garage and into the circular drive. Sparing another scathing glance at his friend, he silently gave thanks for the tinted windows on his vehicle. They couldn't be recognized if they didn't stop anywhere and get out. He could still maintain control over this situation.

Dean tried not to be too obvious while checking for Shannon's minivan in her driveway. He was mildly disappointed when he found it missing. Maybe they'd gone into town. Oh, God—If they had gone into town and he had to introduce Jax ... No, he wasn't even going to think about that possibility.

"See that bakery right there? Best coffee in town. She also makes all her own pastries, so good you want to cry."

"Little old lady?"

"Nah, she's young." Dean shook his head, already knowing where this was going. "Hey, no hookups on this trip, huh? I still have to live here after you come in and break hearts."

Jax tsked, snapping his fingers at the missed opportunity.

"It's a nice little town, I guess, as far as small towns go. I've kept a pretty low profile, but still ... people are friendly, but not in a fake, pushy way. No one recognizes me. And there are no paparazzi. God, I can't tell you how much I love that!"

They had already driven through the main part of town, with all the small Mom and Pop owned businesses. Every sign was handmade. Benches were scattered around. It wasn't as crowded as the beach areas were. The benches were occupied by old men, their arms folded grumpily over their bellies like they were just daring the tourists to claim their spot.

Traffic got heavier as they reached the one-way portion of the road. Dean locked the power window mechanism on his side when he saw the way Jax was drooling over the bikini-clad women strolling along the beach shops. He rolled his eyes. Why couldn't Gage have come to check up on him? Or Toby? Anyone, but the biggest flirt in the band.

Since his friend was otherwise occupied and traffic was at a crawl, Dean focused his attention on his surroundings. He had read that the town was incorporated in the 1600s, and there was evidence of that in the heart of town. But even out here at the beach, it was easy to see that these shops had been run by the same families for generations.

A crowd stood at the window of the candy store. A huge taffy-pulling machine had been placed right there for everyone to see how it was done, right down to the packaging of the saltwater taffy into their little wax paper wrappers. Instead of calling it saltwater taffy, the company called them "kisses." Dean liked the peanut butter kisses the best.

"Check it out, there's a parking spot right there!" Jax was eagerly pointing to an empty space and had even put a hand on the steering wheel to help guide Dean in the right direction.

"Now, hang on. I thought we could drive up the coast a ways and look for some lunch."

"No way, Dino. I came out here to see your new digs. Let's go local!"

Reluctantly, Dean pulled into the parking space and scrounged in his console for some quarters. Jax was already out of the car and nearly bouncing up and down on the sidewalk with excitement. The guy was like an eager puppy. Slowly sliding out of his side, Dean checked in his side mirror to make sure that his disguise was in place. If Jax got him recognized, he was going to kill him.

There was a fried seafood place at the end of the boardwalk. The friends headed that way and got in line to order clams and French fries. Carrying their greasy paper trays overflowing with fried clams, Dean and Jax found themselves followed, not by fans, but by greedy seagulls, waiting for them to drop something yummy. They found an empty spot at the railing and ate their lunch while looking out over the beach. At this hour the sand was nearly invisible, every square inch taken up by towels, blankets, and beach chairs.

Dean popped a fried clam in his mouth and nearly choked when he recognized Shannon sitting in one of the beach chairs near the water's edge. His brain urged him to grab Jax and hightail it out of there before she saw him. His body rooted him to the spot, forcing him to memorize every inch of bared skin exposed by her one piece bathing suit. Knowing Shannon, it was meant to be practical, but to Dean it was sexy as hell.

Maybe she wouldn't spot him. What were the odds that he'd have even spied her on that crowded beach? Before this rational thought could calm his racing nerves, she shaded her eyes and looked right at him. *Crap!* He turned away from the railing as she started to raise her arm to wave. *Crap, crap, crap.* Now she was going to ask questions. Could he just say he hadn't seen her?

He turned slightly, trying to catch a second glimpse. A meaty fist took a hold of his heart and squeezed when he saw the look of hurt on her face. *Oh, Shannon, you don't deserve a jerk like me.* Dean shoved a handful of fries in his mouth and found it really difficult to swallow past the lump of guilt that had lodged itself in his throat.

He was going to suggest to Jax that they start walking when he noticed the woman sitting with Shannon. He knew that look. That was definitely the "I know that I know you from somewhere" look. Crap on a Popsicle stick!

"Hey, Jax, there's a place around the corner that has some really great ice cream. Ever tried blueberry streusel?" Dean got them moving away from the railing and back down the boardwalk. How was he going to get himself out of this one?

• • •

"It's like it's on the edge of my memory. I just feel like I've seen him before."

Talia's words had been buzzing around Shannon's head ever since they'd come back from the beach a couple of days ago. Curiouser and curiouser. And Dean pretending not to have noticed her left a particularly stinging wound. Grouchy with herself and Dean, in equal parts, Shannon swept through the small cottage like a mini tornado.

Her mother was due to arrive any minute. Shannon had offered to pick them up from the airport, as this had been their usual routine until *Roger* came on the scene. She slapped the dampened sponge down on the counter and rubbed hard. "Roger rented us a car, dear. Isn't he lovely?" had been her mother's easy response. Maybe Roger was just as anxious to keep her at arm's length as Shannon was with him.

Good grief! Her mom was pushing 50. She'd gone this long without a man in her life. Why did she have to go and get one now? Shannon stuck her tongue out at the petulant woman pouting back at her from the toaster. She swiped at her image on the shiny surface. She hated feeling like that small little girl who looked up to her mother, who counted on this woman for everything.

Catherine Fitzgerald had taught her daughter the most important thing she had ever learned—that women were not dependent on men to survive. Women could do quite well, perhaps even better, on their own. Thank you very much.

So why change the rules now? Sighing heavily, Shannon tossed the sponge into the mouth of a small ceramic toad sitting on the corner of the sink. She had left the kids on lookout duty in the big picture window in the living room. The squeals coming from that part of the house suggested it was time to put on her big girl panties and meet the new man in Catherine's life.

Shannon and the children spilled out the door and headed for the shiny black BMW sitting in the driveway. Blinking to find the top down, Shannon watched her mother spring out of her side, yank a kerchief off her head, and shake her hair out around her. Laughing merrily, Catherine stooped to gather all three grandchildren into a group hug. Shannon stumbled forward, her gaze focused anywhere but the driver's side of the spiffy sports car.

"Sweetheart, you are looking more gorgeous than ever." Shannon closed her eyes, the scent of lavender and lemon tickling her nostrils. In an instant she was transported to her childhood, remembering the huge overstuffed chair that her mother used to read to her in.

"Mom, I've missed you so much." She breathed in deep, wanting to capture that scent forever, afraid that she would forget it and all the memories it invoked.

"Shannon, children, this is Roger." Catherine beckoned the older gentleman to her side and snaked an arm around his trim waist.

"I've heard so much about you all. I can't tell you how honored I was that you invited me to your home."

News to her! Shannon pasted a bright smile on her face and shook the proffered hand. Roger wore Ray Ban sunglasses, a white polo shirt, and a deep tan. She bet he spent more time on a golf course than anywhere else. Okay, that was petty. The fact that he appeared wealthy shouldn't have rankled the way it did. Her employer was filthy rich and it never bothered her. If she'd met Roger on the street she wouldn't have given it a second thought. Somehow it just made her mother seem more vulnerable.

"I'm so happy you could join my mother for a visit." There, that wasn't too hard.

"Gramma, Gramma, what'd you bring us?" Brenna couldn't hold it in any longer.

Catherine ushered the children back into the cottage, motioning for Roger to bring in one of the bags from the back seat. Shannon stood frozen in the driveway for a moment before rushing to catch up with the others so she wouldn't be left alone with Roger. Remembering her manners, she held the door open for her mother's new friend.

"Mom, are you sure you can't stay here? I can bunk in with Brenna. It's no problem."

Catherine's smile was patient. She left the children playing with their new toys: Brenna with a homemade yarn doll with bright orange hair, the boys with shiny new cars, not unlike the rental that currently sat in the driveway. Roger was telling them about their long plane ride.

"Sweetheart, we discussed this. Roger and I don't want to intrude." When it looked like she was going to be interrupted, Catherine put a hand on her daughter's arm and continued, "We came here to spend time with you all, but we came here to spend some quality time with each other as well."

Oh, please God, don't let that mean what I think it means. Shannon looked up through a narrowed gaze to see her mother's pointed look. *I'm going to have to soak my thoughts in bleach tonight,* she thought. Catherine laughed softly, clearly enjoying her discomfort.

CHAPTER TEN

A soft, sweet ballad floated through the still summer air, strummed on an acoustic guitar. Shannon found herself smiling as she smoothed out the top sheet of the bed she was changing. Replacing the comforter and fluffing up the pillows, she arched her back to work out the kinks. She was ready for Ms. Sheffield and her small army of guests to arrive later that afternoon. Finding herself drawn to the open window, she searched for the source of the beautiful piece.

On the second floor of the large manor, Shannon found that she could look out across the expanse of lawn to the house next door. Unlike this room, its equal on Dean's home had a small balcony. The railing was too high for her to see much except … a pair of bare feet, crossed at the ankle. Dean could play guitar. And he could play well.

Intrigued, she skipped down the stairs and out into the bright sun. Having forgotten to step into her shoes near the door, Shannon, too, was barefoot. The soft grass felt glorious beneath her feet. She looked down and giggled at the sight of her colorful toenails. Brenna had offered to give her a pedicure, painting each nail a different hue. Until then, Shannon hadn't even realized she owned ten different colors of polish.

She slipped through the Arborvitae and into Dean's yard. The guitar still picked out a tune, sad but content at the same time. Shannon followed the music and found herself beneath the balcony she had spotted from the main house. How to get his attention? She coughed. Nothing.

"It's beautiful," she called out.

The music stopped on a discordant note.

"Shannon?"

Dean stood up and peered over the railing. He didn't look happy to see her. She got the sense he felt like he'd been caught. Oh, gosh! She'd intruded on something very private for him. She'd been so enthralled by the music that she was eager to share her praise with him. She hadn't given a thought to his privacy. *Poor Dean! All he wanted was to be left alone and what he got was a nosy neighbor.* Realization had her blushing and stammering an apology. She turned on her heel, head down, the need to escape uppermost in her mind.

"Wait!" he called after her.

• • •

Hurrying through the French doors, across his bedroom and out into the hallway, Dean threw a triumphant sneer at the doorframe that he'd avoided smashing his toes on this time, before missing the first stair tread and almost pitching face-first down the rest of the flight. He refrained from vocalizing the four-letter word he was thinking, but he sure thought it awful hard.

"Shannon? Don't go."

She waited for him on the lawn beneath his bedroom. Toes bare, impossibly long legs in deliciously short shorts, her hair in braids, Shannon was innocence and temptation all wrapped up in one neat package. She looked up at him beneath thick lashes, her bottom lip pinned between her teeth.

"I'm so sorry! I just … I was making the beds, the window was open … it was so beautiful."

"The weather?"

"No, the music." She scrunched up her nose, her expression confused. "I didn't know you played. You're very talented."

Dean watched her closely. She wasn't lying. He didn't know what rock she'd been hiding under, but Shannon genuinely did not recognize him. He thought for sure he'd been found out when she showed up to discuss his music. Her smile was almost shy, her eyes full of admiration.

Something eased inside his chest. Hope, buried for so long, struggled up to the surface. Fear kept him from saying anything stupid. He could never tell Shannon who he had been before. He wanted to remember the way she was looking at him right now. She was seeing him, really seeing him for who he was, not what his celebrity could mean for her.

"You're alone." He'd just realized this and blurted it out, not meaning it to come out as surprised as it had.

"I am." Shannon sounded almost as surprised as he did. She chuckled.

"My mother and her ... friend are visiting. They took the kids to the zoo. I couldn't go. My boss, Ms. Sheffield, is throwing a party at the big house this weekend. I had to finish getting the bedrooms ready."

"I should let you get back to it," he said, though he wanted nothing more than to keep her right there.

"It's okay, I just finished."

She stood there, uncertain, her toes digging into the grass. Bared shoulders revealed a pattern of strawberry-scented freckles that Dean would have liked to explore further. Would they taste as good as they looked? His entire body was a live wire, just waiting to be tripped. *Down, boy!*

"Do you want to come in? I was just going to make some iced tea." He prayed that he actually had the makings of iced tea in his pantry.

"Oh, I don't know. I was just chastising myself for intruding on your privacy." Shannon twisted her fingers together, frowning slightly.

"Please. I'm a horrible grouch. I need you to get on my case. Bug me. Force me to join the land of the living." Dean reached out and untangled her fingers, holding her hands in his and waiting until she met his eyes.

The awareness there, in her gaze, sent fire racing through his veins. Shannon could speak volumes with just those brilliant blue eyes. She was scared, she was vulnerable, but she was hungry. She recognized him as a man. Need flooded his senses, had him hot, hard, and aching in a way he hadn't felt in so long.

Her attention was focused on his mouth. Her dainty tongue darted out to wet her lips. Eyelids lowered, her chest rose and fell as she began to breathe faster. Dean closed the distance between them. Did she even realize what she was asking for? She wanted him as badly as he wanted her.

Letting her hands go at the last second, Dean reached out and cupped the back of Shannon's head. Her lips were already parted, her eyes staring deep into his soul.

"Shannon."

He claimed her mouth, equal parts desperation and tenderness. She moaned low in her throat, her fingers clutching at his shirt. Dean changed the angle of the kiss, eager for more of her. Shannon walked her fingers up his chest until they were curled in the hair at the nape of his neck. Not sure if he'd taken a step forward, she had, or they had moved together, Dean was acutely aware of how closely their bodies fit together.

Breaking off the kiss to nibble his way up to her ear, Dean smoothed his hands down Shannon's back. As the contact became more intimate, he felt the change in her immediately. Her body suddenly stiff, she pushed at his chest, wiggling to get out of his grasp.

"We can't … " Shannon shook her head vigorously.

"I wasn't going to throw you over my shoulder and carry you to my bed. I was just giving in to the moment." His breathing ragged, Dean forced himself not to snap at her. "You going to tell me that wasn't the perfect moment to share a kiss?" He raised an eyebrow in challenge.

"No, it ... I'm not saying ... " Shannon looked as flustered as he felt. She had backed away and was now hugging her arms around her middle.

He'd pushed her too far and now he'd scared her. Feeling like a jerk, Dean gave her the distance she was seeking. Instinct had him longing to draw her into his arms. If he could just hold her until the fear passed. But he knew that, even if it was what she needed, she wasn't ready to admit it. They stood in silence for a few moments, their breathing returning to normal. That bottom lip was between her teeth again. She offered up a small smile.

"What scares you more, knowing I want you or knowing you want me back?" Dean's direct stare was unapologetic.

"I'm not scared." Her laugh was shaky at best.

He waited. Shannon shifted her weight from one foot to the other. Her arms had gone from the protective stance around her waist to hands on her hips, defiant. She stood up straighter. His warrior woman. He fought to keep a grin from forming.

"Listen..." She was shaking her head again. "This can't happen. You and me? I'm a full time mom. I don't have time for ... whatever this is."

"It's your call."

Her jaw slackened. Clearly she wasn't expecting him to back off that easy. This time, Dean did allow himself to grin. He could take things slowly. He wasn't sure if her ex-husband had spooked her or if these were walls that Shannon had erected completely on her own. Dean suspected it had been so long since she had put herself first, that the feelings had overwhelmed her. Oh, yeah, she'd been scared.

"If I promise to behave myself, will you please come in for some iced tea?"

She blew out a deep breath and cocked her head to the side. "You have anything sweet to go with it?"

"I will split my last cranberry orange muffin with you." He spoke this with the reverence it was due. Shannon giggled. "You discovered Cady's pastries, huh?" She headed for the front of the house. "Wait until September and October. I hope you like pumpkin. Oh my goodness, I can taste it now."

Dean fought back a groan at the look of ecstasy on Shannon's face. It was going to be a challenge, holding to his promise to keep his hands to himself. He let her into the house and gestured toward the kitchen, belatedly realizing he was in for all kinds of torture. His eyes were fixed on the slight sway of her hips as she traversed the long hallway. Promising himself a date with a cold shower later, Dean vowed to make the most of this alone time with Shannon.

CHAPTER ELEVEN

"So this neighbor of yours must be really special."

Shannon almost knocked the ice cream from the top of her cone. Her head snapped up, her eyes glazed in a classic "deer in the headlights" look. She wondered if her mother could hear her heart pounding as loudly as she could. She couldn't possibly know about that kiss.

Her mother had always had a way of learning all Shannon's secrets. Shannon took a deep breath and ate another bite of ice cream, a defense mechanism she had learned as a child. She couldn't talk if her mouth was full.

"The children were singing his praises the whole time we were at the zoo. Brady went on about how strong he is. Brian is convinced that Dean is the next Tony Stark. I'm not sure I've heard of him. Is he a sports star?"

Shannon shook her head. She hadn't realized how much Dean had come to mean to her kids. Oh, what had she done? She had all but pushed them into his yard, into his life. And for what, so she could enjoy a little eye candy? No, he wasn't just a gorgeous face. He'd come to mean something to all of them. Absently, she watched the chocolate ice cream dribble down the cone, onto her hand.

" … marry him."

"Whoa! I'm sorry, what?" Shannon leaned over and tossed her melted mess of an ice cream cone into a garbage can. She grabbed the stack of napkins beside her and rubbed briskly at her hands.

"I said, Brenna is already making plans to marry your Dean, once she's grown up. She was telling me all about the flowers and the dress. It sure starts early, doesn't it?"

"He's not my Dean. That's ridiculous! I mean, she can marry whomever she wants when the time is right. But Brenna is too young to be thinking about crushes and marriages and flowers … " Shannon stopped wiping at her sticky fingers when she realized she'd been babbling.

She looked up and, sure enough, Catherine's steely eyes showed she wasn't fooled a bit.

"Oh, baby, what have I done to you?" Tossing her own ice cream away, Catherine drew her daughter up from the picnic table.

"Children, stay with Roger. Your mom and I are going to take a little walk."

The two women left the ice cream shop and walked the short distance to the cliff face, overlooking the Atlantic. They sat on a bench and looked out over the placid ocean. The lighthouse in the distance gleamed white in the late afternoon sun.

"Remember when we used to drive up here and park to watch the storms? There was something so awe-inspiring about the way the waves crashed against the rocks. All that power. You really got the sense that something bigger than us was in charge."

"I remember you telling me that if a boy asks me to park at the lighthouse, it wasn't because he was suggesting we watch the waves. I was to tell him 'No way!' and make him take me back home."

"Uh huh, and instead of following my advice, you jumped at the chance to go with Vincent Bainbridge, the first time he asked you."

"I was merely curious." Shannon felt her cheeks warm at that particular memory. Oh, she'd learned a lot that night.

"But you didn't stay that way." Disappointment tinged her mother's words.

"I beg your pardon? That's like saying you want me to be … unladylike," Shannon stammered. This conversation was making her incredibly uncomfortable.

Catherine sighed, her smile sad. She reached out and took one of Shannon's hands, squeezed. She stared out at the ocean for a long time, like she was trying to figure out how to form what she needed to say.

"I didn't want you to end up like me." She held up her hand when Shannon turned and gave her an incredulous look.

"I let my experience with your father color my entire view of the male population. Men leave. They can't be depended upon. They only think of themselves. They are little boys in a big body."

"I've had my own experiences, you know. Vince wasn't any different than my father. Hell, my dad stuck around longer. Vince cut out as soon as he found out we were having triplets."

"He was young. You were both so young. Have you ever wondered if he would have stayed if you hadn't gotten pregnant right away? Or if you'd only had one baby? I'm not trying to make excuses for Vince, but I think he was just a scared boy. He was overwhelmed."

Shannon frowned, snagging a lock of hair and twirling it absently around her finger. Her mother had never mentioned this before. It would be childish to think the woman was taking sides. To be quite honest, Shannon had just assumed he was looking for an easy way out of a life that had suddenly become one huge responsibility.

"I let my own past influence your view of men … of the world. I made a mistake."

"Mom, that's not true. You were the best parent in the world. You were always there for me. You made me feel safe, loved, protected."

"I sheltered you. I tried to protect you from making the same mistakes I did." Catherine looked up, her gaze somewhere out over the distant horizon. "I was so happy for you when you and Vince said you were getting married. It meant that you were forming your own opinions, taking your own chances. I was so proud of you."

"Is that why you left? Because you thought I didn't need you anymore?"

"My leaving was all about me, sweetheart. It had nothing to do with you. I had put my own life on hold for so long that I almost forgot what it was to be me.

"You were starting your own life, that's true. And it was time for me to find my own way, to finally do something for myself."

Shannon sighed. She remembered the excitement of starting a new life with Vince. But at the same time, she had felt resentment toward her mother for choosing that time to move out to California. She had felt abandoned. To her, her mother was acting flighty, irresponsible. She had never even thought to ask Catherine why she was leaving. Now she understood.

"When you didn't come back after the triplets were born, I thought that was your way of reinforcing that I had to do this on my own. You took on two jobs to support me. You worked so hard to give me the life I had. You did what you needed to do and you didn't ask for help from anyone."

"And I hated it. Oh, my God, there were times I was so bitter, so resentful. I can't tell you how horrible a mother I felt. It is a miracle that you didn't pick up on that." Catherine turned to her daughter, tears coursing down her cheeks.

The sight was too much and Shannon gathered the older woman into her arms, the two of them sobbing on each other's shoulders. So much had come to light. As close as they were, this was a talk that had been too long in coming. Everything Shannon had based her life on, her parenting philosophy on was … skewed.

Scrambling in her pockets for tissues, Catherine sniffled, pulling herself together. She pressed a tissue into Shannon's hand and dabbed at her own tears. They finally made eye contact and both women began to giggle.

"Now, do you want to tell me about your new neighbor? Is Brenna going to have any competition?"

"He's everything the kids say he is and more. He's kind, he's thoughtful, he's patient."

"Is he a good kisser?" Again with the knowing gaze.

"Oh, yeah." Shannon closed her eyes and didn't even bother to hide the pleased smile that took over her whole face. "But I'm not going to ask you the same question. Sorry, Mom. I'm happy you found Roger, or that he found you. But it's just too squicky to think of you … like that." Her expression was half smile, half grimace.

"I won't give you nightmares by offering up too much detail. I just want you to know how happy he makes me. I didn't realize how long I had been cheating myself until Roger came along. He makes me want … more."

"You look happy. Really. I know I'm not used to your having a man in your life, but if Roger makes you look this carefree, then he's got to be good for you."

"I'm glad you think so, baby, because one of the reasons I brought Roger with me was to make an announcement." Catherine's smile slipped a little as she took a deep breath. "Roger and I are getting married."

CHAPTER TWELVE

Shannon shoved her sixth batch of cookies, snickerdoodles this time, into the oven and gave the little plastic timer a sharp twist. Baking always calmed her. Only tonight, that peace was dancing just a tad out of reach. Opening the cupboard with all her plastic containers, she frowned. It was a little late to be worrying about how she was going to pack up and transport all these cookies.

Forget that—who was she going to give them to? The hospital? Too many food allergy issues. Ms. Sheffield had caterers running ragged during her weekend house party, so her guests wouldn't need more food. The 4th of July festivities were tomorrow. Okay. Shannon started to form a plan.

After the parade meandered from the harbor through Main St., ending at the elementary school, the townsfolk gathered in the ball field behind the village fire station. Two different fire stations serviced Scallop Shores, one close to the center of town and one accessible to the beaches. Every 4th of July they held the Fireman's Muster, a series of competitions to see which station reigned supreme. The relay races, tug-of-war, and other activities were bound to stir up appetites. Shannon wiped her hands together and began to collect all the Tupperware and cookie tins she could find.

The timer on the counter and a knock at the front door sounded at the same time. Grabbing a nearby oven mitt, she took the cookies out and turned off the oven. Then she hustled to the front door, groaning when she couldn't turn the doorknob with the hand fitted with the oven mitt.

"So I have to tell you ... " Dean gave the door a little push and brushed past Shannon. "There is the most incredible smell coming from this direction. I figure, as your neighbor, I should investigate. Because there are bound to be people lining up behind me and I wouldn't want you and the kids to get trampled."

"I can't tell you how lucky we are to have you looking out for our welfare."

The calm that Shannon had been searching for through baking was starting to settle in. Was it the fact that she had made a decision to bring the cookies to the Fireman's Muster that had helped sooth her nerves? The other choice was more unsettling. Could Dean showing up on her doorstep be the balm that was easing her bunched muscles and tension headache? Heck, if she dwelled on it too long, the headache was going to come back even stronger.

"Yes, I'm definitely on the right track. It's very close. Please, stay behind me."

Dean held an arm out so that Shannon couldn't even draw up beside him. Half-crouching, he sprang from one wall to another, like he was an FBI agent sneaking up on the bad guy. Shannon found herself a little disappointed that the triplets had already gone to bed. They would have enjoyed this little spectacle.

"I've got it! I can help you make this dangerously delicious smell go away. I offer my services to help eat … " Dean had reached the kitchen and finally got a look at the results of Shannon's baking frenzy. "Ah, hell, even I'm not that hungry."

"It calms me. Or it's supposed to. It was taking longer than usual." The explanation rushed out, the sentences running together in their hurry to escape her mouth. Shannon twisted the oven mitt in her hands, refusing to look Dean in the eye.

"Makes sense to me." He shrugged. "I do get one, though, right? I mean, you can't possibly have every single cookie spoken for?"

"Have as many as you'd like." Tossing the mitt on the counter, she slumped into a chair, drawing her knees up to her chin and wrapping her arms tightly around her legs.

Dean perused the cooling cookie sheets, tapping a finger on his chin before selecting his three favorites. He carried the short stack to the table and sat down across from Shannon.

"You know what would go really great with these? A tall glass of milk."

"If you give a mouse a cookie … "

"Huh?"

Shannon grinned. "Never mind."

She got up, retrieved a glass from the cabinet by the sink and filled it with milk. Setting it in front of Dean, she resumed her position in the chair, dropping her chin onto her knees. Dean lifted the glass in salute and guzzled.

"It's early yet. I figured the kiddos would still be awake, but I don't see them."

"They were wiped out. Everyone was nodding off at the table so I gave them a quick bath and put them to bed early. No one even complained that they didn't get dessert."

"And you've been baking cookies ever since." It wasn't a question, but it was clear that Dean was waiting for the rest of the story.

"And I've been baking cookies ever since."

"Your mom still in town?"

He wasn't going to give her a choice. Shannon scowled. With lightning reflexes, she reached out and snagged his last cookie. Dean's jaw dropped and she swore the sound that he'd cut off had been a whine. She stuck her tongue out and bit into the cookie. Not to be bested, he scrambled up from the table and grabbed another handful for himself, before returning to his seat and directing those soulful green eyes at her.

"Okay, okay. I'll spill." Shannon breathed in through her nose and blew it out slowly. "You sure you don't mind being dumped on like this? You can back out. I don't mind. I'll bake another batch of cookies." The giggle that escaped was nowhere near as lighthearted as she had been going for.

"It's up to you. Either you can tell me your troubles or I can haul you onto my lap and give you the hug you look like you so desperately need." His serious gaze never wavered. Shannon swallowed hard.

"My mom dropped a bomb on me last night. I've been trying to … process it … ever since. I guess I'm not doing so well." She swept the ends of a lock of hair back and forth across her knee like a paintbrush. "So she brought this 'man friend' out for us to meet. You have to understand, my mother has never introduced a boyfriend to me. Not even when I was a little girl and it was just the two of us. I thought she wanted to tell me that she'd finally decided to have a relationship with a man.

"Even that much was tough for me to handle. But I understand that my mom can get lonely and needs companionship. Especially, when she tells me they're staying at a local bed and breakfast. Way more than I wanted to know!" Shannon rolled her eyes, shuddering.

"But last night she tells me they're getting married. I'm not a petulant child. It's not that I'm upset because she didn't ask me first. It's the fact that she is getting married at all. Catherine Fitzgerald is not the marrying kind."

Shannon looked down to see the rest of the cookie she'd stolen crumbled beneath her fist. She stared at the crumbs, afraid to see the look on Dean's face. He must think she was crazy. What sane adult gets so worked up over their parent finding happiness?

"Your parents still together?" She somehow knew the answer would be yes.

"Going on thirty-five years. Every family is different, Shannon."

"I thought we were so alike. I looked up to her. I modeled my life like hers because she was the strongest woman I knew."

"Wait. So falling in love makes her weak?"

"Not weak, vulnerable."

Fear for herself, and fear for her mother had her hand trembling. Could she make him understand? She didn't know why, but it suddenly seemed so important that he understand where she was coming from. Dean's large hand covered her own, the warmth of it sliding under her skin to chase the shivers away. She couldn't take her eyes from their joined hands.

"You're scared she's going to be hurt?"

"Men leave. They stick around for a little fun, but when things get serious they run."

"Forgive me, but if this guy has proposed to your mom, then it sounds like things already are serious. Marriage is a huge commitment."

Shannon scoffed, tugging her hand out from beneath his. "Marriage is nothing. It's easily dissolved. Standing by your significant other and sharing responsibilities, that's commitment. Having the guts to be a dad and help raise and shape your children. That's commitment!"

"Sweetheart?" Dean's voice was soft. "Your mom is in another phase of her life. She's done raising children. She wants to share her life with someone." He leaned in close. "You said you understood that she could get lonely. You said it was just the two of you during your childhood. Would you deny her the chance to grow old with someone?"

"But would it be forever? How do we know? How does anybody know?"

Shannon tried to blink away the stinging behind her eyelids, but all that did was let the backed up tears fall. Sniffling, she swiped angrily at her cheeks. She wished he'd just go home. Why did he have to be so kind? Why was he bothering to listen? Why couldn't he understand how terrifying this was?

A moment's weightlessness was the only warning she had before Shannon felt herself drawn into Dean's arms, draped across his lap. Oh, why did he have to be so perfect? Burying her face in his neck, she registered the fact that he wasn't wearing any cologne. Oddly, this made him even more appealing. He smelled faintly of soap, shampoo, and man. Looping her arms around him and acting on impulse, Shannon flicked her tongue out to taste the spot where his pulse beat strongly.

"Woman, you're playing with fire," Dean uttered gruffly.

His hands began to roam up and down her back. It felt so good to forget. She twirled a finger in the ends of his hair. So silky. His breathing hitched. Emboldened, Shannon replaced her tongue with her lips, kissing her way up the long column of his neck to his ear. Intoxicated by his scent, his very nearness, she drew his earlobe into her mouth.

With a muffled oath, Dean pulled her off his lap long enough to wrap her legs around his waist, before settling down again. He took control, his kiss telling her exactly what he'd like to do with her. Teeth scraping against the tender inside of her bottom lip, he couldn't seem to get close enough. Shannon moaned when his tongue swept in and tangled with hers. More. She wanted more.

"Mommy! I need you, Mommy!"

The sheer panic in Brenna's voice had Shannon scrambling from the warmth of Dean's embrace and jumping into Mommy mode in mere seconds. She spared him the briefest of glances before charging down the hallway.

• • •

Dean stood up, legs trembling, lungs working like a bellows. He ground the heels of his palms against his eyes and then ran his hands through his hair. What the hell had just happened? This woman was going to be the death of him, for sure.

With considerable effort, he finally regained most of his composure. Looking around the kitchen, Dean thought he should probably help put things to rights. There were plastic containers on the counter. He could pack up the cookies. But Brenna had sounded so scared.

Treading softly so as not to wake the boys, Dean tried to figure out which room Shannon had disappeared into. As if on cue, a soft lullaby carried to him from the end of the hall. He stood back from the doorway. Mother and daughter were snuggled in a small bed piled high with stuffed animals.

Shannon's voice was hauntingly lovely. Dean was stunned. She deserved a record deal more than him. She had spotted him peeking in the doorway and smiled softly. "I'll be out soon," she mouthed, rocking Brenna gently.

Nodding, Dean took that as a dismissal and headed back to the kitchen. Strangely, he felt disappointed that he hadn't been asked in to help comfort the child back to sleep. Brenna wasn't his. He had no responsibilities where these kids were concerned. Yet, he found himself wanting to be asked, wanting to be included.

This time he did put the cookies away. Good lord, Shannon had better know what she intended to do with them. There were probably a good six dozen here. Did cookies go in the fridge? Nah. Dean shook his head. Cold cookies were hard cookies.

Looking around, he snatched up the wax paper that lined the counters. He threw it away and began to gather up the dirty cookie sheets and baking racks. When Shannon still didn't show herself, he grabbed a bottle of dish detergent and set to work washing dishes. It didn't take long and he left them to air dry in the plastic rack.

Surely, Brenna couldn't still be upset over whatever nightmare had woken her up? Dean dried his hands on a crocheted dishtowel and hung it back on its hook. He slipped back down the hall and tiptoed into the darkened bedroom.

Shannon lay curled up beneath the Disney Princess comforter, Brenna cradled in her arms. They were both fast asleep. Dean had no idea how long he stood watching them. Fame had taught him that home and hearth probably just weren't in the cards for him. He'd had a lot of time to get used to that idea. But right at this moment, he wanted nothing more than to climb in on the other side of Shannon and hold them both tight.

Swallowing past a hard knot in his throat, Dean backed out of the bedroom. A quick peek in the room across the hall revealed Brian and Brady, snoring softly and safe for the night. He turned off lights as he went and made sure the front door was locked as he let himself out.

CHAPTER THIRTEEN

They couldn't have asked for better weather for the 4th of July parade. Dean rolled the bill of his ball cap to help cut the glare of the sun. He slipped his mirrored shades off his t-shirt and put them on. He was starting to refer to this as his standard uniform. Pathetic. Why couldn't he be like the other guys who had been in the band? They didn't care who recognized them.

What would it hurt, really? People might come up to him and ask for his autograph or a picture with him. No big deal. But it had gotten more complicated than that. There was more at stake. Dean was starting to fall for Shannon, and her kids. He couldn't ruin the possibility of a relationship, not when he was just starting to realize that he actually wanted one.

Hoping to catch a ride with Shannon and the triplets to the parade, Dean had strolled next door. Her smile was apologetic as she explained that her mother and Roger were riding with them and there was no extra room. Still she made no move to invite him in.

It was almost laughable, really. Dean was used to women who couldn't wait to show him off to their friends and family. She may not admit it, but Shannon was making a concerted effort to keep him and her mother apart. Waving a hand in farewell, Dean spun on his heel and headed back the way he'd come.

"Dean?" He paused, glancing over his shoulder. "Thank you for cleaning up the kitchen and putting the cookies away for me."

"It's what neighbors do for each other." He winked.

Shannon had told him they planned to watch the parade from in front of her friend's business, Tumble Tots. He found a parking spot at the elementary school and now strolled down Main St.

looking for the brightly colored building, or three carrot-topped munchkins, whichever he spotted first.

Folding chairs of every style and size lined the parade route. Not all of them were filled yet. The parade started in the harbor, about two miles from this end of town. It wasn't due to start at that end for another half hour, so there was plenty of time to find his neighbors and settle in.

Dean had to do a double take when he noticed someone grilling out of the back of an old pickup truck. Now that was some serious partying spirit! He grinned, wondering if the police on duty would have anything to say about the red plastic cups the grilling group sported. He highly doubted they were filled with lemonade.

Up ahead he spotted the bright yellow building that housed Tumble Tots. Tiny monkeys cavorted in a painted mural on the plate glass window. The window frame had been painted a bright, cherry red. The door was royal blue, with more monkeys on the glass inset. Dean had to admit, monkeys seemed quite fitting.

"Mr. Dean, Mr. Dean!" Brian waved wildly from his spot on the curb. His brother and sister turned and the group jumped up, as one, to race over for hugs.

"Hey there, monkeys. You ready to see some cool fire trucks?"

They bounced around, squealing and giggling. Then they were joined by a pair of identical twins who looked a couple of years younger than their friends. *What did they put in the water supply in this town?* Dean tried not to let his surprise show.

"We're gonna ride on the fire twuck! Mommy said you can come wiff us," one of the twins hollered.

Brady muscled his way to where his mother stood, under the blue striped awning that shaded the doorway. She was speaking to another young mother and dropped a hand on Brady's head, letting him know, without words, that he needed to wait his turn. Dean nearly laughed as he watched the boy twitching with excitement.

She turned to address Brady and the other children. Dean knew the exact moment she spotted him, her jaw dropping slightly, cheeks turning that cute shade of pink. The smile she offered was just for him. Dean wanted to jump up and down just like the kids.

"Who wants to ride on the big fire engine in the parade?" Shannon asked her brood. Dean watched her wince at the shrill response.

"Can Mr. Dean come with us?" Brady had slipped a possessive hand into Dean's.

"I don't see why not." Shannon looked to her friend for verification. "By the way, Dean this is Talia. Talia, Dean."

The woman shook his hand as she watched him closely, the same look on her face as when she had spied him on the boardwalk. The wheels were turning. She knew she knew him from somewhere, but where? Though he wore his standard disguise, ball cap and mirrored sunglasses, Dean swallowed nervously. He ducked his head and tried to resist the urge to dart off into the crowd.

"Hey kiddos, I think I'm going to hang out here. You have a blast, though! I want to hear all about it when you finish the parade route."

Their disappointment was a bitter chorus to his ears. Dean reached out to ruffle each silky head. He wanted to go with them. He really did. But the idea of putting himself out there, for everyone to see, made him want to hurl. His heart squeezed even tighter when he looked up to see the sad look on Shannon's face.

"Well, we can't have Mr. Dean watching the parade all by himself. This is his first Scallop Shores 4th of July parade, after all."

Dean turned to see another small hand thrust out, waiting to be shaken. He blinked. This little tornado must be Shannon's mother. Her grip was strong, her expression warm and welcoming.

He found himself surprised that the woman was not a redhead, like the rest of her family. Her long, wavy hair was quite dark, peppered with strands of silver.

"Catherine Fitzgerald. It's a pleasure to finally meet you." Dean grinned openly when she shot her daughter a look that said she, too, thought Shannon remiss in not having introduced them sooner.

"Shannon, darling, you enjoy the parade with Dean. Roger and I will join Talia, here, in child wrangling. Talia, have I introduced my fiancé, Roger?"

The group started to head for the parking lot at the back of the store. They needed to hurry if they were going to get the kids to the fire trucks, lined up and ready at the other end of the parade route. Brenna tugged her hand from her grandmother's and dashed back to Dean.

"We get to throw out kisses to the people watchin' on the ground. I'm gonna throw mine right to you. So you catch 'em, okay?"

"You've got it, Princess." He resisted the urge to gather her up and settled for a wink. He laughed when she returned it with one of her own.

"You're going to have your hands full with that one." He nodded at the little girl jogging off, pigtails jiggling as she went.

"She only has eyes for you, you know?" Shannon looked up at him from beneath her lashes.

"She's got good taste for someone so young." He feigned pain when she punched him in the shoulder. "What? It's my cross to bear."

The lighthearted repartee was cut short when Shannon suddenly frowned. Her attention was focused somewhere across the street. Dean tried to see what was causing her distress. Leaning against a lamppost was an older gentleman, a green plaid sunhat clashing with the salmon colored polo that stretched across his ample middle. To say that he was sneering was putting it mildly. This guy was definitely looking right at Shannon, and the hatred on his face was unmistakable.

"Come on. Let's find a better place to view the parade. I want to be closer to the school when the kids get off the fire truck." She grabbed his hand and began to walk quickly.

"Shannon, who is that guy? 'Cause, first impression? He looks like a jerk."

"That is my ex-father-in-law." She kept walking, her eyes looking straight ahead, shoulders rigid. "And, yes, he is a jerk."

• • •

It felt like a huge cloud now blocked out the sun. Shannon shivered. She stopped walking, closing her eyes when Dean drew her close, rubbing her bare shoulder. He knew just how to make her feel better. For the briefest of moments, she let herself lean into his touch. If she were a cat, she might have purred.

"What was that all about back there?" His voice was soft in her ear.

"Don't worry about it. We're supposed to be having fun, right?" She flashed him a smile that she hoped looked genuine. Dean's frown told her she'd missed the mark.

"I'm not trying to be pushy. I know it's none of my business. But, Shannon—" He tugged her off the sidewalk, into the shadowed doorway of the real estate office. "That guy had hate written all over his face."

"You noticed that too?" She leaned against the door, trying to brace herself against the nerves that threatened to rattle her teeth loose.

"How did things end? Do you mind talking about it?"

"To be honest, it didn't really involve Hollis. I don't know what that guy's issue is." She reached for Dean's hand again. "Let's go snag that spot under the big oak."

Their end of the parade route was finally beginning to fill up. Children lined the sidewalks, waving small flags. Behind them were rows of chairs, two deep. Then there were the shop owners and their families, hanging out in their doorways. For a small town, the 4th of July parade had an amazing turnout.

Shannon and Dean sat beneath the mighty oak, digging their heels into the soft grass, so as not to slide down the slight hill into the crowd in front of them. She took off her backpack, rummaged inside, and drew out a couple bottles of water. Dean took his and tapped it against the other bottle in cheers. She took a few swallows, gathering her thoughts.

"We were high school sweethearts. We didn't think anything would tear us apart. Then college acceptance letters started coming in." Her smile turned wistful. "I got into Lyndon State in Vermont. Vince got into USM, just an hour away."

"You gave up your own dreams to help him follow his."

"All I wanted to do was be a teacher. Not exactly a lofty career ambition. Vince was going to be a doctor. He was going to be somebody." Shannon was surprised to realize that her voice still held that same touch of pride, defensiveness for her old flame.

"By the time we found out we'd be in different states, it was too late for me to apply for the fall semester at USM. When he found out I was willing to drop my college plans and follow him up to Portland, Vince melted. He said he felt so honored." Shannon plucked a blade of grass, rolling and unrolling it over her finger.

"We got married that summer, just before school started. My mom was happy for us, but a little worried that we were starting life so young. Vince's parents didn't care for the fact that their son was marrying so early, but as long as he remained focused on his studies, they let it go.

"I got a couple of jobs waitressing so we could afford an apartment just off campus."

"And what did Vince do?" Dean's voice was gruff, low.

"He studied. He kept his grades up." Shannon shook her head, raising her shoulders in silent question.

"So when was it your turn? When did you get to start your college career?" Dean turned her to face him. Shannon tried to laugh off the question, but the laughter got caught in her throat when he slipped a finger under her chin and forced eye contact.

"We never had enough money for me to take classes. It was all earmarked for Vince. Vince had the future. I could always go to college once he got his career established. Then I found out I was pregnant. We were thrilled. He was thrilled—really. It was May and Vince had just gotten out of school for the summer. We were looking forward to bonding over the summer with my growing belly." She smirked.

"He came with me to the ultrasound. I was ten weeks along. We were hoping to hear the baby's heartbeat." Dean seemed to sense that this is where things started to get rough for her. He pulled her into his arms.

"The technician found a heartbeat, then another … then another. I was in shock, completely blown away. Multiples didn't run in either family. I looked up at Vince. I was scared. I needed his reassurance that we could do this." Shannon scooted ever closer, wanting nothing more than to climb inside Dean's skin and share it with him for a while.

"The look on his face, it was like Vince had completely shut down. I couldn't figure out what he was thinking. But the man who had been looking forward to a baby, a single baby, was just … gone."

"Oh, sweetheart." Dean dropped a kiss on top of her head and rubbed her back. He would have continued to hold her like that, but Shannon needed to finish. She pushed against his chest and wiped at an errant tear. His expression was so compassionate. She dropped her gaze, knowing if she continued to look at him she was going to completely lose it.

"Anyway, I had a shift that afternoon. I got home late, after midnight. Vince was gone, all his stuff cleared out. He'd left a note. He said he just couldn't do this. He had plans, a future. He couldn't let anything get in the way."

"Wonder what his future patients would think of their fine, upstanding doctor if they knew his backstory." Dean scrunched up his nose. "Wait. Is he still studying to be a doctor?"

Shannon thought for a moment. "I'm not sure, to be honest. He'd have his undergraduate degree, for sure. He should still be in medical school. Frankly, I have no idea where he is now." She took another swallow of water and tried to wrap up her sob story.

"I came home and had the babies here. I tried to reach out to Hollis and Eden, Vince's parents. I thought they might want to be a part of their grandchildren's lives." Her cheeks flamed as she remembered that particular exchange.

"Hollis accused me of trying to pimp my children for money. He told me that if I contacted them again, that he would take out a restraining order on me. That there was no way I was going to get my greedy hands on his family money."

"Ah, so that winning personality definitely runs in the family." Dean looked inordinately pleased that he'd gotten a smile out of her.

Shannon heard the first faint whoop of a fire engine. She scrambled to her feet and hauled Dean up beside her.

"Okay, now that I've vomited up my past, let's just drop it." She flashed him a pained smile and swung her attention to the road in front of her.

They moved in close with the rest of the crowd. Shriners in their little maroon fezzes drove by in impossibly small cars, looping around in crazy figure eights. Shannon watched Dean's face light up with delight. It was fun experiencing something that had been an annual event for as long as she could remember with a person seeing it for the first time.

Local Boy Scout troops filed past. Daisies, Brownies, and Girl Scouts were interspersed with marching bands, Veterans from as far back as WWII, and a collection of muscle cars. Dean clapped for everyone, but Shannon could almost see the drool starting to form when a vivid yellow Corvette purred by.

"I bet I know what you're going to ask Santa for this Christmas." She giggled.

The antique models of fire trucks began to roll past and Shannon stepped a little closer, trying to get a clearer view of the road. The triplets would be passing them any minute now. She bounced on her toes, eager to see her excited children.

"Hurry, hop on." Dean had crouched down in front of her to offer a piggyback view.

Giggling girlishly, Shannon wrapped her arms around his neck and sprang up onto his back. Dean held tight to her thighs, both of them laughing so hard they nearly toppled. The largest engine drew up close and Shannon waved her arms high in the air, hollering each triplet's name. She saw the moment they spotted her, their bright smiles dazzling. Her mother waved from behind them, one arm around Roger.

"Mommy, Mr. Dean! Have a kiss!" Brenna's aim was spot on and Shannon reached out and caught the taffy without losing her balance. She blew them a kiss of her own.

The fire engine signaled the end of the parade, volunteer firemen following behind with a long, thick rope. Shannon slid down Dean's back and they hurried off to the elementary school, where the group of children was to be unloaded.

Seeing Hollis Bainbridge had put a damper on the day for Shannon, but talking about her past wasn't as difficult as she would have thought. Maybe time was healing those old wounds.

Or maybe it was the quiet, patient way Dean had listened to her story, never judging her choices. He jogged alongside her, clearly just as eager to meet up with the children as she was. A tiny, hopeful part of her wondered if this is what it was like to be a family. The idea was thrilling and terrifying at the same time.

CHAPTER FOURTEEN

Dean sat cross-legged on the floor in the children's section of the town library, forgoing his ball cap and shades for the first time, and not feeling the slightest bit nervous about being around people. He waited for the clenching stomach muscles, the cold sweat whenever he accidentally made eye contact. It didn't come. He was doing this. And more importantly, he was enjoying himself.

His grin huge, he glanced over at Shannon, who sat beside him. The triplets were huddled together in the very front row of little people. Miss Bree, the librarian, was putting felt pieces of food up on a big black background, as she told her audience about the Very Hungry Caterpillar.

Dean had never heard this story before and found himself leaning forward. What a great idea—to not just tell a story, but to show it! He wondered if Miss Bree would let him play with the felt board after story time. He turned and flashed a grin at Shannon. He thought of the Madonna as he watched her. She only had eyes for her children. The pride, the joy that lit her face, it was humbling.

The festivities from the day before ended up running late into the evening. Dean had offered Roger and Catherine his SUV to take them back to the bed and breakfast. He said they could bring it by any time today. The triplets had talked him into coming in to read them bedtime stories. One book had led to another and Dean found himself invited to story time at the library. Did those kids ever get a "no" for an answer?

Oh, boy, now they were on their feet singing "Head, Shoulders, Knees, and Toes." Did anyone else's knees crack as bad as his? Shannon giggled out loud, which could only mean she'd heard. He stuck out his tongue, tempted to tug on one of the braids she'd wrangled her hair into.

"Remember, next week we're going to read about families. Moms, dads, brothers, sisters … You're welcome to bring in a photo of your family if you want to share it with the group."

The children all clustered in front of Miss Bree's chair. Dean tried to get a look at what the fuss was about. The librarian's brunette head was barely visible in the sea of preschoolers. Shannon's laughter reminded Dean that he was being rather obvious.

"Did you want to get your hand stamped too?" she asked sweetly.

"Oh, is that what's going on?" He sighed wistfully.

"What were you expecting? She gives out gifts at the end?" Her smile was indulgent.

"Hey, cut me some slack. This was my first story time." This time he did reach out and yank lightly on a shiny, red braid.

"Mommy, Mr. Dean, lookit what I got! Miss Bree gave me a fish stamp." Brian proudly showed off the blue fish stamped on his left hand.

His brother and sister crowded around them and stuck their little fists out as well. Shannon made suitably impressed oohs and aahs. Not sure what to do, Dean reached out and tousled the boys' hair. Brenna slipped her tiny hand into his, beaming up at him in adoration. Oh, the power she wielded when she flashed that smile. Her mom had an equally powerful one.

"Should we head home so you can get your car back?" Shannon nodded toward the door.

"Nah. I told them to take their time. I don't have anywhere I need to be."

They said goodbye to Miss Bree and wandered toward the shelves of age-appropriate picture books for the kids. Dean watched them, tapping spines, rubbing their chins, and looking so contemplative, he had to stifle a grin behind his hand. Shannon was right beside them, reading off titles to the books that the kids found themselves drawn to.

"Have you gotten a library card yet, Dean?"

The question gave him pause. At the height of his career, he'd never had time for libraries. He'd grab a paperback from the airport souvenir shops. It wasn't that he didn't read.

"I hadn't thought of it. I used to read a lot on the bus. We'd pass a paperback along until all of us had read it."

"All of us?"

Crap. "Uh. You know ... in high school."

"There is a terrific bookstore in town, the Book Nook. The old woman who owns it, Ruby, is a sweetheart. But libraries fit in much better with our budget, if you get my meaning." Shannon held up a large stack of books.

Dean reached out and took them from her. She rounded up the troops and headed for the check-out kiosk. He watched in wide-eyed amazement as the children took turns scanning the bar codes on the cover of the books. This machine was even better than the felt board.

Outside, the sun was being stingy, at best, but the humidity kept the temperature plenty warm. They tossed the library books into the van and walked up the street, no destination in mind. The triplets skipped ahead, mindful not to put too much distance between them and the adults.

"So the other night ... you were pretty upset about your mom getting remarried." He left the rest unsaid, ready to be told to mind his own business.

"I freaked, didn't I?" Shannon smiled, but it still looked a bit forced.

"If you'd run out of ingredients for cookies, would you have started making a fruit salad, or a crock pot stew?"

She laughed. "I would have switched to my other calming technique. I can crochet a scarf in about an hour, you know."

"Ah, well in that case, I like all shades of blue." He winked.

They followed the children to the small playground at the end of the street. As the triplets dashed in three different directions, Shannon and Dean found an empty bench and parked themselves.

Brady had long-since learned how to compensate for the cast on his arm. Dean noticed the slight tensing when Shannon saw her son taking chances. But he had to hand it to her, she didn't say anything. It was probably killing her not to warn them all against doing anything dangerous, but she kept it all in.

Brenna had found another little girl on the swings and they had struck up that instant friendship that only the very young could pull off. Brian was at the top of the monkey bars, little muscles straining as he swung his way to the end. Dean leaned back and smiled. He had the strongest urge to pull Shannon up against him, so they could watch the kids together.

"Oh my God. That's my mother and Roger."

She pointed to a couple coming out of an antique store, hand in hand. They stopped just outside the store and kissed. The gesture was so tender, so real. Dean smiled wistfully. He had the ability to step back and view them as the loving couple they represented. Shannon, so personally involved, shuddered.

"Try to pretend they were just a couple of strangers. Look at them as if you were just seeing them for the first time."

"They look happy." She tore her gaze away. "They look in love."

"You going to give them your blessing?"

"She didn't even ask!" Then, grudgingly, "Yes. Of course they have my blessing."

Shannon leaned back against the bench, her shoulder resting against his. She pointed at Brian zipping down the slide to land in a giggling heap at the bottom. He gave her a thumbs-up as he raced off to his next destination. It was such a peaceful day.

"I'd watch out around this one, if I were you. She'll ruin your life. I've seen her do it before. She's a family wrecker."

Dean's head snapped up at the intrusion. Shannon's hand grabbed his, icy cold and trembling. The nasty jerk from the parade stood over them. His eyes were full of bitterness and hatred. Dean was torn between wanting to defend Shannon's honor and wanting to keep this a quiet, private conversation.

"This isn't the time or place, pal. You want to talk about whatever you *think* Shannon did, you and I can meet up somewhere."

"She's poison. Those kids, though … " He turned a calculating gaze toward the playground. "Vincent is in a good place now. He's turned his life around. I bet if he could see his kids, he'd be proud. Proud enough to come back. Proud enough to visit his poor ma."

They watched the older man as his calculating eyes darted from one little redhead to the next. He wet his lips and appeared to be forming some kind of plan in his head. Shannon whimpered. He whipped his head back and sneered at her.

"Vincent deserves to see his kids, spend time with 'em. You can't hide them away from him forever."

"He's the one who left! He didn't want to have anything to do with them." Her voice was shrill and panicked.

Dean stood up and closed the distance between himself and Hollis. The man was a good four inches shorter. He took a deep breath and tried to look as menacing as possible. The triplets were starting to pay attention to the conversation the adults were conducting and he needed to end this before they could overhear.

"No one is interested in your opinion. You had your chance years ago. Not my problem if you blew it." He stared down the old man, daring him to blink first.

"Vincent is ready to come get his kids. He's wanting to make up for lost time." Hollis spun on his heel and stalked from the playground.

Mustering the brightest smile he could manage, Dean waved at the kids, silently encouraging them to continue playing. They returned his wave and went back to what they were doing. He sat down beside Shannon and pulled her close. Her shuddering gasps told him she was fighting off tears—hard.

He raised his head and checked out the direction he'd seen that detestable man head off in. Across the street, he spotted Catherine and Roger. Her lips were pursed and she was staring at Shannon. She must have seen what had happened. He wanted to be able to smile off her worries, but he knew better. Catherine was a mama bear and he almost felt sorry for the man if she decided to go after him.

• • •

A summer squall had everyone dashing down the street for the minivan. Dean held out his hand for the keys and Shannon didn't even have the strength to argue. She slid into the passenger seat and left Dean to make sure the kids were all buckled in. It was taking everything she had to keep it together.

They drove through town and then continued on toward the beaches, missing the turnoff for the harbor and Shannon's cottage. Dean turned up the heat and flashed her a bolstering smile. She held her hands out to the vent and swallowed a sob when they wouldn't stop shaking. Her breaths were slow and measured.

"Don't let him win. This is what he wants. He wants to see you rattled, miserable. Don't give him the satisfaction."

"Please just take me home." She wouldn't even look at him.

"I will, eventually. But right now it's lunchtime and I think today is a great day for pizza. Who's with me?"

The triplets hollered their approval from the backseat. Shannon hugged her arms against her body and shook her head hard. "We can't. It's not ... I can't afford it, Dean."

"And that's totally fine, because I wasn't asking you to pay. I brought it up and I plan to treat."

The windshield wipers slapped rhythmically as they continued the trip in silence. Everyone seemed to have long since taken cover, the sidewalks and the road strangely deserted. Shannon slowly began to relax. Dean was right. If she had gone straight home, she would have put a movie on for the kids and then given in to a major tear fest under cover of the shower.

"Fine. I like pepperoni and mushroom." She spared him a half smile.

Dean pulled the van into the half empty parking lot of Polly's Pizzeria. Shannon was mildly surprised that he had discovered this place on his own. It was well off the main drag. But then again, he was a guy ... and a single guy at that. They had a built-in pizza and beer radar.

She was actually grinning by the time she got out of the car and helped the triplets down. They raced to the front door and out of the rain. Shannon waited until Dean caught up to her and then silently mouthed "thank you." His expression unreadable, he nodded.

Since it wasn't very crowded, Shannon let the kids get their own table. She left Brenna refereeing an arm wrestling contest between her brothers. She sat at one of the tall tables, where she could keep an eye on her brood. Dean put in their order at the counter and then joined her at the table.

The rain was no longer coming down in buckets, but it wasn't ready to pack it in either. Shannon watched a rivulet of water snake its way down the window, passing through both the P's in Polly and Pizzeria. She turned away from the window to see Dean studying her.

"How are you doing?"

"I'm okay. More pissed than anything else. No one threatens to take my kids away from me."

"That's my girl."

Shannon blushed at the remark. She knew he hadn't meant it that way, but a tiny part of her couldn't help but wish he had. She bit her lip and darted her gaze elsewhere.

"Shannon? Shannon Fitzgerald?" The waitress had brought their food out already.

"Hey, Megan James, right? How have you been?"

"I've been getting old in my parents' pizza joint, that's what." She giggled. "I haven't seen you in ages. Are you living in town?"

"Yep, moved back to have the triplets." Shannon nodded at the table they sat at.

"Oh, goodness, yes. My mom told me you'd had triplets. And don't they look just like you! So, Vince, are you the big doctor you said you were going to be when we graduated?" The waitress clapped a hand over her mouth, her eyes gone wide. "I'm so sorry. You are *not* Vince."

"I lost touch with Vince after our divorce." Shannon's apologetic smile encompassed both Megan and Dean.

"Okay, so we know I'm still working here and living with the 'rents. How about you? Did you get your teaching degree? You had a scholarship, right?"

Shannon snorted. She had been awarded a scholarship that would have paid for her textbooks that first year. She'd hardly call that a scholarship.

"Nah. The triplets keep me hopping. I'm the caretaker for one of the manors up on the Bluff. Pretty sweet deal."

Megan set down their pizza and drinks. She set the tray on her hip and gave Dean a saucy wink. "Well, Vince's loss. I'd say you've traded up, girl." She gave them a short wave and spun on her heel.

This time it was Dean's turn to blush. He coughed, presumably to hide his embarrassment, and reached for the same slice of pizza as Shannon. As their hands touched they locked gazes, just for the briefest of moments. Her breath hitched in her throat as she watched his irises darken with lust. She had to fight the urge to lean in just a little closer and see what might happen.

"Mommy, I brought our plates. Fill 'er up please!" Brian's carrot top only came up to her knee in these tall chairs. He held a stack of paper plates up so she could reach them.

"Go back and sit down. I'll serve you guys." Shannon began to load plates and slid from her seat to deliver them.

"Hey, bud, go long!" Dean held a small paper carton of milk and let it fly before Shannon could squeak out a protest. "What?" His face a portrait of childlike innocence, Dean held his hands up, palms out.

Brian had caught the milk, thankfully, but now his brother and sister were lined up waiting for their milks to be delivered in the same method. Dean looked over for her approval, grinning devilishly when she rolled her eyes and shrugged.

Shannon turned to see if their waitress had seen how close they had come to a major spill. Megan was grinning behind the counter, flashing a thumbs-up sign when they made eye contact. Shannon chuckled. Her stomach rumbled as the garlic, oregano, and tomato sauce assaulted her senses. Diving in, she pulled a slice from the pie, licking her lips as the cheese clung stubbornly to the rest of the pizza, stretching in long strings.

"Good call, Neighbor. Good call." She groaned around the first bite.

CHAPTER FIFTEEN

Dean snapped his laptop shut with a little more force than necessary. He slid it back on the desk and made room for his elbows. Groaning, he massaged his temples with his fingertips.

His lawyer was pushing for a court date on the paternity suit. Dean was still holding out hope that this woman would drop the charges when she realized he wouldn't settle. She didn't have a chance in hell. Her kid was only a year old. Since Dean had given up sex over two years ago, her case was groundless.

But just like the rest, she had to try. She wanted a piece of his money, his fame. Why should he have to prove his innocence, time and time again? If anyone should be proving anything, it was that woman.

Dean pushed out of his chair and stalked toward the kitchen, his goal the last cup of coffee in the pot. Most people would be kept awake, drinking coffee this close to bed. But the warmth of the liquid sliding down his throat soothed him, smoothed out his frayed nerves.

He carried his favorite mug, a Kermit one his mom had given him for Christmas years ago, out to the deck. The humidity wasn't bad after dark, and the night was still warm. Dean listened to the crickets in the grass and the soft sound of the waves hitting the bluff. His nose picked out the lingering scent of charcoal and burgers. Shannon had barbequed for dinner.

As he closed his eyes, the steam rising from the coffee tickled his nose. He took that first sip and felt it all the way down to his stomach. Yes, coffee had a calming effect on him. He smiled. Shannon had suggested this local brand. Logan's Bakery carried it by the pound. Cady Eaton, the manager, had definitely snagged a lifelong customer in Dean.

Shannon consumed his thoughts, yet again. A piece of Dean understood that she was part of what calmed him, what redirected his focus from upsetting things. But he wasn't ready to admit that. She scared him. Okay, to be more precise, his feelings for her scared him. She made him want things he had no business wanting. She made him want to trust again.

He set his mug down on the patio table and slumped into the chair. He couldn't ever tell her who he was. It would kill him, the changes he'd see in her. He knew she and the kids were hurting for money. He'd be more than happy to help out where he could. But if she knew who he really was, what kind of bankroll he came with, she'd look at him differently. She'd start wanting things.

Would it be so bad if she wanted things? Was it possible that there was a woman out there that Dean would willingly give everything he owned just to be with? He thought about his old band member, Toby. Toby was married now, had a little boy. No, things were different for Toby. Vanessa wasn't a fan that he'd met out on the road. She and Toby had known each other since they were little kids. She'd been there to support him right from the start of his career.

Dean glanced at the house, thinking about another email he'd read that evening. Some stupid reality show wanted to reunite all the boy bands from years past. This was what Jax had been trying to talk him into. Jax missed the fame, the women, and all their attention. Dean would be happy if he never had to step into the spotlight again. Couldn't they do this without him? Wasn't there always one difficult band member who went into seclusion and refused to be bothered? That was him. Please just let that be his role.

He was really starting to enjoy life in Scallop Shores. At first, he had intended to really live the hermit's life, only coming out for provisions when he absolutely had no choice. But Shannon had convinced him that he couldn't live that way. Once he realized people weren't going to attack him in the streets for autographs and pictures, he began to explore.

It was a beautiful, old, historic town. Someday, he was going to have to take the historical society's tour of the tavern, the old Gaol, the schoolhouse, and the wharf. But since he'd arrived just in time for tourist season, he was getting to know the beach areas before they closed up for the winter.

Then what? If he was going to put down roots, stay in Scallop Shores permanently, he had to find something to do with his time. Dean got up and began to pace the length of the deck. This was his thinking pace—head down, concentrating. Not to be confused with his stressed pace—agitated and faster, treading just a little bit harder across the smooth wood boards.

Would it tip people off if he were to give guitar lessons? He was proficient in all sorts of music and instruments. Did he qualify for a teaching position at school? Forget it. That was probably locked in by some old guy who wouldn't give it up until he croaked. Besides, he'd have to let the school in on his background. He couldn't do that, could he?

Dean's pacing led him to the door and back into the house, his Kermit mug abandoned on the patio table. He'd been writing songs, even sold a few. But what could he do that would ensure that he didn't slip back into his hermit shell? Something that got him involved in the community.

Shucking his jeans and t-shirt, he slipped under the covers with a notebook and pen. Propped up against pillows, Dean jotted notes and made lists until his yawns nearly cracked his jaw. He tossed the writing supplies onto the pillow beside him and wriggled his way to a prone position. *Just can't let Shannon figure out my other life*, was his last thought before succumbing to slumber.

...

"Oh my goodness, you look so adorable!" Shannon hugged her friend Quinn, smiling wistfully at the woman's huge belly.

"Counting down the weeks now. Only four more to go until these two make an appearance." She rubbed her rounded tummy with one hand while reaching for her glass of lemonade with the other.

"So does Jonah still want to name them Luke and Leia?" Talia asked.

"Yes, and Lily wants to name them Mickey and Minnie. You see what I'm up against?"

The women all laughed.

Talia and Jeff were hosting a barbeque and had asked Shannon to bring everyone—her mom, Roger, and even Dean. The kids had raced off to play with the twins and their friend Lily. The men were clustered around the huge gas grill having a serious discussion—about meat? Sports? Who knew? She was happy to see that Dean looked at ease. He usually seemed to be on edge around Talia, but today he was fine.

"How did you know you wanted to open your own business, working with kids?" Shannon posed her question to Talia.

"Why? You thinking of taking on entrepreneurship?" Her friend cocked her head to the side.

"No, not really. Well, I don't know." Shannon trailed off, her brow crinkling.

Catherine scooted her chair closer so she could get in on the conversation. Quinn was leaning forward as well. She'd gotten their attention.

"I was thinking about college—finally starting, you know? But that seems so daunting. I'm not eighteen anymore. I don't even know where to begin."

"But you're thinking about it." Catherine's eyes were shining. "Do you know how long it took me to get to where you are now? My baby was all grown up before I started to think about having a life, a goal."

"Mom, it's no big deal. I'm still thinking about the kids. I'm thinking about their financial future."

"But you need something for you, something that's all your own. It's what gives your life purpose." Talia was nodding excitedly.

"Well, I guess that's the crux of it, right there. Only I don't know where to begin."

"You wanted to teach, right? Do you still want to do that?" Catherine asked.

"I do. But a four-year degree, and then student teaching and … it's so overwhelming. When would I find the time to go to school? Who will watch the kids while I'm studying?"

"There's a teacher's aide position opening up at the elementary school. One of my clients teaches first grade. She told me the number of incoming students this year is much higher than last year. She's put in for an aide to help with the child to teacher ratio, and she isn't the only one."

"Don't I need a degree for that?"

"You need a high school diploma, for sure. I think they ask for some college credit, but it can't hurt to try. Especially, if you let them know that your ultimate goal is to become a teacher."

"Life experience goes a long way, my friend, and when they know you are single-handedly raising triplets, they will beg you to take the job." Quinn patted Shannon on the knee.

Pulling her lip between her teeth, she thought about working at the elementary school. She wouldn't have to quit her job managing Ms. Sheffield's estate, because her boss very rarely needed anything after Labor Day. A good thing, too, because Shannon and the children lived rent free in her cottage. She didn't know what they were going to do when she did, finally, decide to give up this job for something more permanent.

"I've been so used to spending every waking moment with them. If I have to rattle around that big manor house all by myself while they're in kindergarten, I'd go insane." She took a deep breath. "I need this."

Dean's laughter rang out from the other side of the deck. Shannon turned her head, their gazes colliding. He held on tenaciously, like he was daring her not to break eye contact. Then he winked. Incorrigible! A small smile on her face, she refocused on her own conversation, hoping the other women hadn't noticed.

They had. Of course. Shannon's mother was beaming, her approval of Dean and a possible relationship readily apparent. Talia was flashing her a "just do it" grin. Shannon rolled her eyes and tried to keep the blush from taking over her whole face.

"Bright Starts has openings for before and after school care, if you need them. They're right across the street from the school. Lily loves it there and her teacher is the sweetest thing." Quinn's smile was encouraging.

"Oh! And they run on the Scallop Shores school district schedule. So they're closed on the same days you'd be off," Talia added.

Well, she certainly had a lot to think about. Shannon tucked her legs beneath her in her chair, and reached for her beer. She took a long sip, cradling the bottle in her hands while she played casual observer.

Her mom had gotten up from the table to join Roger, the two drifting off to enjoy a quiet conversation away from the rest of the group. Talia had left for the kitchen, tossing the salad and getting ready to serve dinner. Jeff flipped steaks, burgers, and hot dogs. Shannon could see that most had been taken off the direct flame. They'd be eating soon. She chuckled when her stomach rumbled loudly enough to be heard the next town over.

The boys were all wrestling on the grass and it took Shannon a moment to spot Dean. He was sitting beneath a shade tree. He held a clutch of dandelions and sat patiently while Brenna and Lily tucked some more behind his ear. He looked so ridiculous and so ... hot. Shannon groaned.

When the triplets were really little, she'd tried to imagine what Vince would have been like with them. But that had just been a depressing reminder that her children didn't have a father figure in their lives. Their father hadn't wanted them. He hadn't wanted her enough to stay.

She had tried to be everything to her kids: mother, father, doctor, and teacher. By this point she'd gotten so good at being everything to them that she hadn't stopped to wonder if they really were missing something. Watching Brenna chattering away as she decorated Dean, she worried that her daughter was pining for a father.

They looked so cute together. It would be so easy to let her imagination run wild, to fantasize about a future that involved Dean. He would be such a good dad. Not every man had those instincts, least of all any man she'd ever met. Dean didn't even seem to realize this about himself.

But fantasies like that belonged in romance novels. Real life didn't come with guarantees. Real life was cruel. Counting on someone else to stick around and play happily ever after only led to disappointment. Shannon had learned that the hard way. She wasn't going to fall for it again. She tore her gaze away from the cozy scene, shutting out the fantasy trying to take root in her heart.

"I'm only here for a few more days. If you don't take advantage of that and go out with your gorgeous neighbor, you are a fool."

Catherine spoke quietly but purposefully in her ear. Shannon didn't need to turn to see the stubborn set to her mother's jaw. She just knew that it was there, the expression that was on her mother's face. That "don't-mess-with-me" look had gotten Shannon to do her chores, finish her homework, anything that Catherine expected of her daughter, without argument. It was for her own good, of course.

"Mom, I'm not a kid anymore. You can't tell me what to do."

"You know that's not what I'm trying to do. I'm pushing you out of your comfort zone and you don't like it." She sat down opposite Shannon. "Tell me you don't want to go out with him."

"We don't have a future."

"I'm not talking about the future. I'm talking about one night, alone, no kids. Go catch a movie. Go skinny dipping at the pond. Go back to his place and have your wicked way with him. Be happy. Be a woman, Shannon. Enjoy some one on one time. Enjoy ... Dean."

"Oh, my God, Mother!"

Now it was all she could do *not* to picture Dean naked. This was too much! She was going to kill the woman ... right after she took advantage of her babysitting services so she could go out with her neighbor. Or stay in. Great. Now she was a ticking time bomb. A drooling, ticking time bomb who couldn't stop picturing her next door neighbor naked.

CHAPTER SIXTEEN

"Do you have any wine?"

Shannon stood in the doorway, nearly soaked to the skin from her jog through the rain. Shivering in front of him, she clutched a picnic basket with white knuckles. Dean held the door open, waited while she crossed the threshold, and peered out to see if the triplets were with her.

"Wouldn't you rather have some coffee? Or tea? You must be freezing." He took the basket from her and started to head back to the kitchen.

"Wine would be a more appropriate date beverage."

Her words stopped him in his tracks and Dean turned to spear her with a heated stare. Shannon swallowed hard, standing tall. Her chin was tipped up, her eyes sparking. He was confused. Had they made some kind of plans that he'd forgotten? No. If they had planned a date he would definitely remember.

"Who's watching the kids?"

They were standing in the hallway, the narrow confines suddenly feeling even more cramped. Dean rubbed the back of his neck with a hand. It might be pouring outside, but the house suddenly felt like the inside of a furnace. Or maybe it was just him.

"My mother. She's leaving tomorrow." She dropped her gaze to the buttons on the front of Dean's shirt. "I was told I should take advantage of this opportunity." There went the bottom lip between her teeth.

"Ah, I knew I liked your mom." He took a step closer. "So you brought me dinner?"

"I was going to cook for you. I'd planned to bring the ingredients and maybe give you a cooking lesson."

Dean cocked an eyebrow, waiting.

"But they're talking about possible power outages, especially along the coast. I figured we could have a picnic in front of the fire, just in case we lose electricity."

That heat surrounding them in the hallway went from blazing to inferno. Dean hoped he wasn't visibly sweating. He watched Shannon's throat bob as she swallowed. He liked making her react. He liked knowing he affected her on a sexual level.

"Then, by all means, let's get a fire started." He smiled wickedly when her eyes went wide as saucers.

"But the lights are on. We can still eat at the table." Shannon tried to tug the picnic basket from Dean's grasp.

He covered her hand on the basket's handle with one of his. Leaning in close he spoke softly in her ear, his words low and gruff.

"I thought this was a date. If this is the kind of date I think we're talking about, then it calls for a fire in the fireplace. Wouldn't you agree?"

He was glad she was here, but he wanted to make sure they were on the same page. This was Shannon's chance to keep the tone of the evening lighthearted and casual. *Please say yes.* He held his breath, his eyes riveted to her plump red lips.

"I … it does, yes."

"But?"

"No, no buts. I'm nervous, is all. It's silly. I haven't been on a date for a very long time."

Dean appreciated that she didn't mention Vince's name. She was trembling in her damp clothes. He needed to get that fire cranked up. He took her by the hand and pulled her with him into the cozy den. There was a fireplace in the more formal living room, but the space was so huge that Shannon would have to wait much longer for the heat to soak in.

He grabbed a thick throw off the Lazy Boy and laid it out in front of the fireplace. With a flick of a switch, a gas-lit fire whooshed to life. Ah, modern conveniences! Shannon didn't wait for an invitation; slipping her shoes off at the door, she scooted across the blanket and reached her hands up close to the glass surface of the fireplace.

"Oh, this is … heavenly." Her sigh sent tiny electric shocks straight to his groin.

"I'll go get that wine," he croaked, walking stiff-legged to the kitchen.

Dean grabbed a couple of wine glasses from the cupboard and set them on the center island. He'd had this foolish grin on his face ever since he'd answered his door to find the wet, bedraggled woman shivering on his doorstep. Did she realize how huge this was for her? She was finally putting herself first.

Contemplating a dry Chardonnay and a bold Cabernet Sauvignon, Dean put them both back. Shannon's mother was leaving tomorrow. This was their only chance to spend some time without the kids. They were going to celebrate. He dug out the champagne he'd been saving to celebrate winning the paternity suit and popped the cork.

Did he have champagne flutes? Would she care? Dean tamped down the anxious flutters in his stomach and told himself not to find excuses to delay joining Shannon by the fire. He snatched up the glasses he'd already set out and carried everything to the den.

Shannon had opened the picnic basket and was setting out plates. Dean settled down beside her, sneaking a peek into the basket. She pulled out a plastic container of strawberries, as red as her lips. Dean swallowed. She handed him a serving spoon and a larger container. He tugged at the corner and sniffed. A light vinaigrette. Cold pasta salad with grape tomatoes, olives, and cucumbers.

It was like some magical basket, with no bottom. Shannon was still taking out containers and placing them on the blanket. How they all fit in there, he couldn't figure it out. A cheese platter. Assorted types of crackers. Bite size brownies. Dean had to resist snatching one of those before they'd even eaten their main meal.

He realized she'd finished and was sitting back, watching him expectantly. She handed him an empty plate. Licking his lips, Dean began to pile it with goodies. He plucked a strawberry from the container, picturing himself feeding it to Shannon, and almost dropped it. Easy, boy!

"Like I said, I was trying to think of something we wouldn't need the stove for. I hope you like everything."

"Are you kidding? I was going to sit down and watch the game with a bowl of Lucky Charms."

"Oh, my gosh! I didn't even think. I'm keeping you from the game. I should go."

"Shannon." He set down his plate and cupped her knee with his palm. "This," he waved his hand to encompass their little spread, "trumps a baseball game—any day."

She nodded shyly and went back to filling her own plate. They ate quietly, for the most part. Dean stifled a groan when Shannon sucked on the tip of her finger to clean off some dressing. She nibbled at crackers, while he popped them in his mouth whole.

"Tell me what it was like growing up in Scallop Shores. What's winter like in Maine? Is it as bitter cold as we hear about in California? What's it like to live through a hurricane?"

Shannon angled her feet toward the fireplace, wiggling her bare toes. She accepted the sparkling wine from Dean, sneezing when she stuck her nose too close to the bubbles in her glass. Then she giggled.

"Scallop Shores can get pretty boring in winter. When I was growing up, we lived closer to town. The boys on our road would play hockey as soon as the ice on the pond was safe. There was a girl a few years older than me. Wynter. I know … ironic. We were the only girls out there on the pond. She was so patient, letting me tag along with her everywhere. She taught me to ice skate.

"Then there were the big hills out on the golf course. We used to love to race each other down on sleds. After a good snowfall, I swear I'd see half the town out there. Living out here on the Bluff, when the roads get icy and snowy, it's best to just stay put."

"Should I buy a snowmobile? Can you teach me to drive one?" He was only half-joking.

"Wouldn't be a bad idea." Shannon chuckled.

They drank their champagne and watched the flames dance in front of them, blue at the bottom and getting brighter and lighter as they reached the top. Shannon began to gather up the dirty dishes and pack them back into the picnic basket. Dean hurried to help, hoping his eagerness wasn't as pathetically obvious as he figured it was.

He picked up the basket and set it off to the side, away from the blanket. Then he got up and pulled some big pillows from their hiding place inside a large ottoman. He carried them to the blanket and set them up so they could both lean back and enjoy the view of the fire.

Refilling his wine glass, then hers, Dean realized he was putting off the inevitable. He was nervous. It had been a long time since he'd been with a woman. He'd had his pick. He could have been like the other guys, enjoying the perks of the job and sleeping with a different woman every night. Maybe he was just weird, but he didn't like the way girls threw themselves at him.

Call him traditional, but Dean liked to be the one to initiate intimacy. Then why did it thrill him so much that Shannon had just shown up like this? They both knew what they were expecting. Truthfully, he was probably looking for something a little more permanent than she was. God, this was crazy! Shannon had him crawling out of his skin with want for her. He just didn't get this hot and bothered over women. He had more self-control than that. Well, he used to.

Shannon leaned back against the pillows and stretched her long legs out. Skimpy cut-off jeans accentuated her golden summer tan. Dean could no longer think coherently. His whole body was beginning to throb in time to his pulse. He needed to kiss her. He needed to touch her. He needed to be inside her.

• • •

She hoped he didn't realize how fast she'd guzzled that last glass of wine. Shannon swallowed hard and stretched out her legs, trying, for all the world, to look like a relaxed, carefree woman. *Play the seductress*, she thought. Then just as quickly she wondered, *What does a seductress do?* She fought the urge to get up and call the whole evening off.

"I'm really glad you came over." Dean reached down for one of her hands, rubbing his thumb over the knuckles.

"I was afraid you'd think I was too forward."

"That would imply that this was all a calculated plan on your part." He squeezed her hand and smiled softly. "I get the feeling that it took a lot for you to be here tonight.

She should have felt embarrassed that Dean had seen through her so easily. Instead, his smile set her at ease, made her want to stay. He offered to refill her champagne again but Shannon shook her head. She didn't want to be fuzzy-brained. She wanted to remember this night.

He stood up, carrying the bottle and both wine glasses over to a small table, out of the way. Shannon watched his movements, the way his muscles bunched beneath his shirt and his soft-as-butter jeans. She knew the moment he caught her watching, but she continued to look her fill. When she got to his eyes she shuddered.

Dean knelt down in front of her, holding her gaze captive. His irises were dark, full of passion. She wet her lips and snuck a peek at his mouth, that full bottom lip just begging to be sucked on. She was shaking, she realized. Whether from fear or need, she wasn't certain.

"You can trust me."

There he went, reading her mind again. She took a deep breath and held it, reaching out to cup his cheek in her hand. His face was rough, stubble scratching her palm. She gasped when he took her hand and placed a soft, slow kiss into the center. She let her breath out on a long sigh.

"Wait! I brought something." Shannon reached into the pocket of her cut offs and pulled out a foil wrapper.

"Only one? Well, now I'm disappointed," Dean teased.

Shannon's cheeks flamed as he took the condom from her shaky fingers and laid it on the blanket. She hated that she felt so awkward, so unschooled in the ways of lovemaking. If this was going to be the only chance they had, at least for a very long time, then she wanted to make it as perfect as possible.

He moved in close, nuzzling her neck and pulling her against him at the same time. Shannon shivered as his fingers skidded up her bare arms, raising goose bumps as well as her body temperature. Their mouths fused, lips searching, tongues tangling. She felt drunk with power, feminine power, when raking her nails down his back elicited a deep, rumbling moan. She wanted to see what else he liked.

Emboldened, she reached for the top button on his shirt and undid it, revealing warm golden skin that just begged to be kissed. All doubts aside, Shannon continued to undress Dean, letting go just long enough for him to pull her damp t-shirt over her head.

Just as he was lowering them both to the floor, thunder boomed loud enough to shake the walls, and the electricity went out. They froze for a few seconds, never breaking eye contact. The flickering flames from the gas fireplace gave off the only light in the room. She couldn't have asked for a better way to set the mood.

Dean finished removing their clothing. Shannon held out her arms for him. They lay side by side on the blanket and she sensed he was giving her a chance to chicken out. She stretched a thigh out, covering his leg, and brushed it higher and higher still. Dean closed his eyes, a wicked smile on his face.

"Do you know how long I've wanted to find out if you taste as sweet as you smell? Wild strawberries. It's been driving me crazy." His tongue swept out to lave her collarbone. "Mm ... even better."

She squirmed beneath him, realizing with a bashful horror where he intended to take those dizzying licks. She dug her fingers into his longish locks, trying to slow his descent so she could talk him out of it. It wasn't right. Vince had never ... Oh! He tugged a taut nipple into his mouth and the suckling sensation drove all coherent thought from Shannon's brain.

"Dean," she whispered, her back arching to offer more of her breast to his greedy mouth.

He switched to the other side, not stopping until her left breast was just as achy and tingling as the right. Dean had been distracting her, knowing her better than she knew herself. Now he continued on his journey south and she was a puddle of sparking nerve endings who couldn't lift a finger to stop him, even if she wanted to.

"So much sweeter," he murmured against her fevered skin.

His tongue drove her to frenzied heights, causing her to cry out in ecstasy. She hadn't even known pleasure like this was possible. Her body was singing Dean's praises.

She was startled to realize that he'd awakened some sort of monster. She couldn't get enough. Her body still thrumming from the aftershocks of a shattering release, Shannon needed more. She needed to feel him stretch her, fill her. She would beg if need be.

"Please." Her voice was a keening whine that held no resemblance to anything she'd uttered previously in her life.

His answer was immediate, rising up to cover her body with his own. She cried out as their bodies joined, clutching him tightly to her. She wanted to sob, with relief, with need, with a surge of emotion she didn't quite know how to express. They moved together as one, their bodies working in perfect syncopation. He anticipated her needs before she could vocalize them. She knew, by his soft grunts, his tensed muscles, and his unfocused eyes that she was giving as good as she got.

They both reached the pinnacle of pleasure nearly simultaneously. Dean cupped her face in his hands, locking that emerald gaze with hers. She'd trusted him with her body, and now she knew it would be all too easy to trust him with her heart.

Afterward, she lay with her head pillowed on his chest. She listened to the heavy drumming, slowly returning to a normal rhythm. Lightning flashed outside, the room still only illuminated by the gas lit fireplace. Shannon smiled the sleepy, slow smile of a woman well satisfied.

She spared a brief thought for the triplets, now fast asleep in their beds, safely watched over by their grandmother. This moment was hers. All these years, she had always thought that she would regret sharing herself with anyone but her children. But she was wrong. Maybe she'd been waiting all this time for Dean.

"What are you thinking about?" His words tickled her ear as she heard them reverberating through his chest.

"I'm happy. I put myself first and the world didn't stop."

"Well, we did blow out the electricity." He tickled his fingers slowly down her bare back.

"Oh, that was our doing, huh? Aren't we the power couple?" Shannon squeezed her eyes shut, frowning. She'd just gone and ruined the carefree moment by throwing in the "c" word.

"That we are." Dean kissed the top of her head. His tickling turned to deliberate stroking and Shannon felt the hard evidence of his interest in a second go 'round.

She blinked. Why wasn't he put off by her last comment? "Too bad we only had the one condom." He sighed wistfully. "Okay, I may have a couple more in my other pocket." Shannon peeked up at him.

"Bless you, my wicked woman." He dumped her unceremoniously on the blanket while he scrambled up to root through her discarded clothes.

Well if he wasn't going to throw her out for referring to them as a couple, then she was going to stop obsessing over it. Live in the moment. Live for herself. Dean cheered, holding up two more foil wrapped packets triumphantly.

It looked like they were going to make the most of this night. Shannon hoped her mother didn't mind snoozing on the couch. She didn't think she'd make it back any time soon. She squealed when Dean pounced on her.

CHAPTER SEVENTEEN

"I believe a 'thank you, Mom' would be in order."

Catherine sat in the front seat of Shannon's minivan. Her eyes were focused on the ribbon of highway in front of them. Her lips twitched at the corners, where the ghost of a smile played hide and seek.

"I told you thank you last night."

"Yes, but you look just as radiant this morning so it can't hurt to say it again."

Shannon rolled her eyes and tried to will the heat in her cheeks to cool down. She glanced in the rearview mirror to gauge whether or not the kids were paying any attention to the conversation going on in the front. Nope. Brenna was busy coloring, a handy tray over her lap. Brian had a zillion tiny cars on his tray, crashing them this way and that. Brady was playing the alphabet game … by himself. He watched intently out the window for his next answer.

"I really appreciate your watching the kids last night. I'm glad you all got some last minute alone-time together." Shannon sent a pointed glance at her mother.

"It was my pleasure. Well, it was probably yours too." Catherine bit on her knuckle to stifle a giggle, but not before she let a snort escape.

If they hadn't been doing 65 miles an hour down I-95, Shannon would have beaten her head against the steering wheel. The woman gets a sex life after a twenty-year dry spell and she develops a teenager's crude sense of humor.

"So did Roger get back and settled in safely?" Shannon was desperate for a change in subject.

"Yes, yes, he's very sorry he had to leave early."

"It was completely necessary. I hope everything is all right."

Roger had gotten a call the day before about a break-in at his house. The police needed him there to assess damage and catalog what had been stolen. Catherine had offered to change her ticket and leave early as well, but he'd insisted she spend what little time she had left with her daughter and grandchildren.

They passed a few more exits in silence. Shannon's mind wandered to the evening before. She'd been disappointed when the lights eventually flickered back to life. She had enjoyed their date far more than she'd expected. Today she was relaxed, pleasantly achy, and longing for the next glimpse of her incredibly sexy neighbor.

"Hey, Mom, when you met Dean, did you think there was anything strange about him? When I first met him, I could swear there was something he was trying to hide. Now I'm not so sure." Shannon frowned in uncertainty.

"Now I wish you'd said this before. I'm trying to remember my first impressions." Catherine tapped a finger against her chin.

"I remember thinking, 'Did Malibu Ken get lost and end up on the opposite coast?'" She chuckled.

"But in town, at the parade … " Catherine stopped tapping her chin and stabbed at the air in front of her instead. "He looked nervous then, like he was afraid of being recognized. But who would know him in Scallop Shores, right? Yeah, that seemed a little weird to me."

Shannon nodded. He was much more at ease with her and the kids now. It was only when he was in town that he donned those ridiculous mirrored sunglasses and ball cap. Like he was some kind of celebrity, trying to remain undetected. Sure, he was gorgeous enough to be a model, but she'd know if he was someone famous. Right? She sighed. Now who was acting strange?

"Sweetheart, I need to be straight with you about something. It's actually good that Roger isn't here for this conversation."

This time both women checked to see that the triplets were still occupied. When she knew that all little ears were tuned elsewhere, Shannon glanced worriedly at her mom. Catherine looked embarrassed, on edge.

"Are you okay? Are you sick?" Her heart began to beat too loudly and she was afraid she'd miss the answer for the pounding in her ears.

"It's not me. It's you." Catherine shook her head, clearly frustrated with how she was handling this conversation. "I saw Hollis Bainbridge talking to you at the playground the other day. You never mentioned it, but I was hoping you'd tell me what he said."

"Oh, Mom, he's so hateful! He was telling Dean to stay away from me, that I ruin lives. That I ruined his son's life and, by extension, his and Eden's."

"What a bastard! Did he say anything else?"

"He said he'd been talking to Vince and that he'd told him about the triplets. That Vince was interested in being part of their lives. He implied that Vince was going to take them away from me." She was speaking in a whispered hiss but the emotion behind the words had the sentences coming out in choked pieces.

"Hollis is just messing with you. He knows what would scare you the most and he's using it to make you miserable." Catherine flattened her head against the back of the seat and closed her eyes. "This is my fault," she whispered.

"That's crazy. He's had it out for me ever since his son freaked out over fathering triplets and ran."

"Yeah, well, he's had it out for me—and by extension you—since I told him to get his cheating hands off me, that I would not have an affair with him!"

Again, they both checked the backseat for eager listeners.

"You're kidding me! Hollis Bainbridge? Oh, that's just … ew!"

"What can I say? I was hot stuff."

Shannon grinned, thankful for the comedic interlude. However, it was short-lived.

"Promise me you won't let him near those children. I'm not saying he'd do anything to harm them, but he's got a mean, vengeful streak. Two Fitzgerald women have pissed him off and who knows how far he's willing to go to assuage his manly pride."

"I appreciate your telling me this." Shannon smiled sadly at her mother. "Kind of makes me wish we could just pick up and move out to Carmel with you. Get away from Scallop Shores and Hollis Bainbridge."

"You run away from him, you are no better than Vincent. Stand strong and let him know you don't take crap from anyone. You're a Fitzgerald." They reached out and squeezed their fingers together.

"Besides, you have a smokin' hot neighbor that, I have a feeling, would miss the heck out of you—and the kids—if you were to move."

"And that's your polite way of saying 'I staked out Carmel, go get your own damned spot,' right?"

"Didn't say that."

"Didn't have to." Shannon grinned as she bore right for the exit to the airport.

• • •

Dean paced back and forth, his cell phone clenched tightly to his ear. They shouldn't have done this. Why couldn't they just accept that he wanted no part of any reality TV show, reunions, or anything that required getting on a plane and stepping out of his anonymous bubble?

"Hey, Jax suggested I come in person. He said you have this thing for your hot, single mom neighbor. He said if I brought

Vanessa and the baby, that maybe we could convince you to come back. Just to tape the show, man. Then you're free to go."

"Toby, you've got a normal life now. You have a wife and a baby. You do the 9-5 thing. Don't you feel that it's enough?"

"I'm not doing this TV gig because I'm jonesing for the old life. It's just a lark. Something my kids will get a kick out of when I'm older, and no one asks us to do reunion shows anymore. Because, you know, eventually they won't want us anymore. The public, not our kids." Toby chuckled.

Dean sighed, letting all the air out of his lungs before refilling them. He grabbed a handful of hair and tugged. This wasn't going well. They just weren't hearing him.

"I can't do it, Tobers. I've got too much to lose."

He thought of Shannon, the look on her face if she happened to flip on the TV and catch his ugly mug on a show about boy bands past. She'd hate him. She'd read him the riot act about how she had trusted him and how he betrayed that trust. And she'd be right. He'd deserve every ounce of loathing.

"Does this have to do with your neighbor?" Toby asked, suddenly serious.

"I lied to her, man. I guess you could call it a lie by omission. She doesn't know who I am. And I don't want her to. It would change things. It would change us."

"Does she have something against boy bands? Get her heart broken when her fan mail wasn't answered?"

"No, you ass! It's not her. It's me. I've never met a woman who didn't act differently the minute she found out I was famous. They start calculating. They're picturing themselves with my last name, thinking of all the checks they'll be able to write."

"Ouch. You are one jaded pop star. You're really clueless if you think that all women are that greedy and manipulative." Toby tsked.

"You're lucky. You've got Vanessa and she's great. But do you ever wonder if you guys had met after you got famous, if things would have been different?"

"Vanessa is Vanessa. When you fall in love and really get to know someone, you know they don't change, their core principles don't change, just by adding a little bit of money."

Dean stopped pacing and considered this gem. He didn't want to think badly of Shannon. He couldn't picture her as anything but generous and nurturing, giving of her time, energy, and affection. He had everything exactly the way he wanted it. Maybe he was being unreasonable, but that cold, gnawing fear just wouldn't let go.

"If you see a future for you and this woman, you need to be truthful with her. Does she know about that frickin' sham of a paternity suit?"

"No." His voice was glum. "I'm evil, okay? I lied to her about who I was. I left out the part about the crazy chick crying 'Daddy!'" Dean paced up to the wall and thudded his head against it. "Toby, if you only knew how devoted she was to her kids. She's ... they're ... "

"You want the whole package." Now it was Toby's turn to let out a long sigh. "Maybe I *should* come out there. You're delusional. You need an intervention to show you just how bad you're screwing up your chances with Ms. Perfect here."

"Don't you dare! Shannon can't find out about you guys."

"Tell me something, Dino. If it weren't for her, if you didn't have to worry about anyone accidentally spotting you on TV and having your cover blown, would you do the show?"

"Why do you need me? Surely, they don't need all five guys to show up for this reunion thing? Tell them I died."

"You didn't answer my question."

"If it would get you off my ass, then yeah, I'd probably go out to film the stupid thing and then *hasta la vista!*"

"So tell her. Set yourself free, man! Tell Shannon the truth and then ask her to join you in LA for the show. Fly her kids out, too. How many does she have?"

"Three—triplets, actually."

"Jesus."

"Cutest damned kids you'll ever see." Dean wondered at the pride in his voice. Where did that come from?

"Yeah, well I'm looking at the cutest kid in the world right now, and his purple face is telling me I've got to cut this call short. Daddy's got some nasty business to attend to."

"You have fun with that. Be happy you only have to change one at a time."

"Dean? I'm serious. Bring her out to meet us. She sounds like a damned decent lady and you deserve someone like that in your life. Love you, man."

He ended the call and shoved the phone deep in his pocket. Like it was that simple. Things were complicated now. They were lovers. She'd gone to him thinking she knew everything there was to know about him. She'd trusted him with all of her. If she found out now, she'd feel betrayed on a whole new level.

Dean went back to pacing the floor. Shannon. He wanted to be the man she thought she knew. He wanted to be honorable, honest, and forthright. But he also wanted to be hers. He wanted her to need him. He wanted her to love him. Every day he got to spend with her, it was getting harder and harder to keep this from her.

Toby was right. He needed to tell her the truth. His Shannon wouldn't turn weird just because she found out he was a celebrity has-been. And if she did turn out to be a gold digger, then it was better that he found out before it was too late, right? Before he lost his heart. Right... Who was he kidding? It was way too late for that.

CHAPTER EIGHTEEN

She was going to die. Shannon clutched the box of tissues to her chest and stumbled down the hallway. Well, that was only if she were really lucky. Sometime in the night she had started to feel bad—really bad. Now she had to face the truth: she had the flu.

The kids had gotten up at 6 o'clock, full of energy and ready to start their days' adventures. She'd considered letting them fix their own breakfasts, but three five-year-olds in the kitchen sounded like way too much of a disaster in the making. So she'd gotten out of bed.

Now she was struggling with all she had just to make it until she could get back to bed. Ms. Sheffield was bringing a group of guests out tomorrow morning. Shannon had a to do list she'd been adding to for days. She had hours of work ahead of her and she couldn't even get her achy body out of her pajamas. She blew her nose into a tissue and leaned against the wall. She wouldn't cry.

"Mommy, can we go out and play?" Brian hopped up and down, forcing Shannon to squeeze her eyes shut against the havoc his energy was wreaking on her equilibrium.

"I was hoping I could get a few helpers at the big house today. Mommy's not feeling well."

Brian stopped hopping and slumped. He dragged his feet and sighed dramatically.

"Can we just play for a few minutes? Then we'll help. Pinky swear."

Shannon waved him outside, trying for a shaky smile. "No one gets hurt today—you hear me? I'm too sick to drive you to the hospital." She shook her head when her order was met with giggles. *They think I'm kidding.*

Shoving her feet into a pair of bright pink flip-flops, Shannon headed for the big house—in her pajamas. Who was she going to run into? Ms. Sheffield wouldn't be around until the next day.

She got the cleaning supplies out of the huge utility closet in the garage. She groaned, thinking about all the windows that needed cleaning and how badly her whole body already hurt. How was she going to raise her arms above her head when she could barely shuffle across the lawn to get to the house?

Shannon took a few deep, slow breaths. The aching in her head was so bad she was afraid she was going to vomit. But then she'd have to clean it up. So that just wasn't going to happen. Oh, she really didn't have time for this!

Honking into a tissue, she shoved it back down into her pocket. Shannon turned a bleary gaze to the window. She knew the triplets were out there—she'd heard them just a few minutes ago. But where had they gone? She pushed herself away from the windowsill and turned back to the vacuum. She'd go round up her escapees after she finished vacuuming the downstairs.

She was halfway through the living room when she heard the children over the sound of the vacuum. She shut it off and turned, ready to chastise them for tracking dirt in on their sneakers. All three children stood proudly, pushing Dean to the forefront of their little group.

"You said you needed helpers 'cause you weren't feeling well. So we went and got Dean." Brian beamed.

Shannon looked from her own bedraggled bedhead and rumpled pajamas to Dean's tight white t-shirt and navy cargo shorts. She burst out crying. Dean knelt down and whispered something to the kids, who turned and filed out of the room. Then he hurried over to Shannon, who stood blubbering in the center of the room, her teeth chattering. He placed a cool hand on her forehead and silently swore.

"God, baby, you are burning up. What the hell are you doing over here? You should be in bed."

"Can't. Too much to do." She hugged herself tightly, trying to keep from biting her tongue when she couldn't control the shivering.

"You're no good to anyone like this. You can't do everything. In fact, today, you can't do anything." He placed a finger over her lips when she started to protest. "That's an order."

He lifted her in his arms like she didn't weigh a thing and carried her to the couch. Shannon lifted her head off the pillow he'd placed beneath her and tried to get up. A wave of vicious dizziness had her stomach pitching dangerously and she decided it wouldn't be in her best interest to fight him.

"You tell me what needs to be done and the trips and I will do it. You will stay here and rest. Get some sleep if you can." He covered her with a homemade afghan he'd found draped on the couch.

Shannon nodded weakly.

"I have a list on the kitchen table. The kids know where all the supplies are kept." She sniffled. "Dean, I'm so sorry."

"For what? Getting sick? I highly doubt you did it on purpose." He dropped a kiss on her fevered brow and started to leave the room.

"Do you need me to bring a bucket?"

"No, I'll be okay." Mortification added to the bright flush on her cheeks. Of all people to have to see her like this.

Shannon drifted in and out of sleep, roused by the occasional bang of a cupboard or the muffled giggle of one of the children. She alternated between kicking off the blanket because she was too warm and hauling it back over her when the chills began anew. Dean had left a box of tissues within reach and she was quickly filling the small wastebasket with crumpled tissues.

It was lunchtime and she really needed to get up and fix something at the cottage for the triplets. She had just managed to stand and fold the blanket on the couch when Dean walked in. He shook his head when he saw she'd disobeyed orders.

"Sit down. As soon as I finish vacuuming this room we'll be done."

"But my list?" she sputtered.

"Work goes fast when you split it between four people. I imagine it takes a lot longer when you insist on doing it all yourself." He lifted a brow and sent her a pointed stare.

"It's my job," she moaned. "Who am I going to ask for help?"

"I bet this job doesn't come with benefits like vacation or sick days, does it?" He frowned.

Dean turned on the vacuum and made short work of the rest of the carpet. Shannon sat obediently on the couch, lifting her feet when he needed to vacuum underneath them. When he was done, he returned the vacuum to the utility closet, came back for his patient, and carried her all the way back to the cottage, the children leading the way. Shannon was too miserably sick to argue.

• • •

The aching in her head had eased off enough to where she was no longer so worried she'd hurl all over her houseguest. She sat up in bed, propped up against pillows, sipping weak tea. She'd tried to have Dean drop her off on the couch but he insisted she be put straight to bed. His only concession was to let her remain sitting, so she could pretend, at least, that she was somewhat involved in the care of her children and household.

Giggles and chatter reached her ears from the kitchen. It was lunchtime, but what that consisted of today, Shannon had no idea. All Dean had to do was look in the fridge or the pantry for any number of easy-to-make choices. She tried to keep lots of healthy things on hand. It's possible they could be eating their way through a bag of potato chips, but she had to trust that Dean would be more responsible than that.

It killed her to just sit here and do nothing. She was a doer. She worked through pain and illnesses. She didn't have any choice. She'd never had help. This was hard for her, humbling. And yet she knew her kids were in good hands. She could trust Dean to help out while she was sick. She was almost starting to believe she could trust him to stick around no matter what. Maybe the fever was making her delirious.

"I brought some crackers and broth. Wasn't sure you were up to anything more filling, but I can fix you something if you'd like."

Dean carried a tray into the room, followed by the children. They were unusually subdued. Shannon glanced from them to Dean, frowning slightly.

He shrugged a shoulder and flashed her a grin. "I told them they could come with me if they promised not to jump up and attack you in bed. It might jiggle your stomach too much and make you throw up. And then they'd have to clean it up."

Shannon smiled at the horrified looks on all three faces. She whispered a "thank you" to Dean and patted the bed gently.

"I'd love some company as long as you can sit gently."

The triplets' whole demeanor changed when they were told they could stay and visit. With huge grins and exaggerated care, they climbed onto the bed and gave their mother careful kisses. She closed her eyes and breathed in the scent of her sweet babies.

Dean was still standing beside the bed and Shannon tamped down an unbidden thrill that he was in her bedroom. She swore the man really must be able to read minds because, when she looked up at him, he winked. Cheeky!

"Mommy, we had quesadillas for lunch. Mr. Dean cooked 'em for us."

"An' he let us sprinkle the cheese on."

"We wanted lemonade but he told us we had to have milk, 'cause it makes your bones and teeth strong."

"Well, I guess you don't need your old mother today, then. Mr. Dean is taking good care of you."

"Yeah, but we said we needed hugs and he said he thought you probably needed some right back."

"He was very right about that."

Shannon reached her arms around until she had each child within her grasp. She laid a kiss on each temple, smoothing back their bangs and checking foreheads to make sure that no one was coming down with what she had. When she was satisfied that they were all well, she let them go, shooing them off the bed so Dean could set the lunch tray down.

Having assured themselves that their mom was just sick but would be back to herself in no time, the kids dashed from the room. Off to the next adventure. Dean set the tray across Shannon's lap and lowered himself to the bed beside her.

"So the preferred method for gauging a fever is this?" He leaned in and swept her hair from her forehead, his lips feather light against her skin.

"You shouldn't. I don't want you to get sick." She lowered her head to duck out of his reach.

"But you'd take care of me, right?"

"Of course!" Wow, that came out a little too forcefully. Shannon squirmed from embarrassment.

"That makes me very happy to hear." He wrapped an arm around her shoulder and drew her close enough to drop a kiss on the crown of her head.

He slipped off the bed and gave his patient an assessing gaze. She straightened her back and tried to give him a cheerful smile. He shook his head and backed toward the door.

"Nice try, but you need sleep. I'm going to go clean up the kitchen and then the kids have challenged me to a water balloon fight. I promise we'll keep it outdoors and everyone will have bathing suits on."

"Leave it. The kitchen. I'll clean it when I get up."

"Sorry, sweetheart, but I'm in charge today. Your only job today is to get better. In order to do that, you have to rest. Don't make me get my bossy pants on!"

Shannon nearly snorted out the soup she'd just taken a sip of. Bossy pants. Is that what she sounded like on a normal day? Good grief.

Dean waved from the doorway and headed back down the hall. The kids were playing in the living room, no doubt waiting for Dean's permission to escape to the beautiful summer day outside. It was blessedly quiet in Shannon's room.

She found a blister-packed pill that promised daytime relief for flu symptoms under her napkin. *Bless you, Dean!* She tossed it back with a sip of water and moved the tray to her bedside table. It was time to let go, put things in someone else's hands and just sleep. The last thought she had before succumbing to slumber was Dean, in a frilly apron and nothing else. Ah, the beautifully colored world of a drug-induced sleep.

• • •

Dean's nose smelled the brewing coffee before his ears could register the sound of the coffeemaker churning out a delicious pot. His eyes still closed, he breathed deeply. Not just coffee. He sniffed again. Bacon. Oh ... and something covered with maple syrup. He'd died and gone to heaven.

He opened his eyes and looked around groggily. Last night, after he had put the kids to bed, he had gone back to his place and packed an overnight bag. He wasn't sure how long Shannon would be doped up on cold meds and he wanted to be there if the triplets needed anything in the middle of the night. So he'd camped out on their living room couch.

As he slowly came to wakefulness, Dean could hear hushed whispers coming from the kitchen. They were letting him sleep in. It must be killing the kids not to be chattering at full volume, running around and jumping all over him. He was touched. He threw back the quilt he'd discovered in the hall closet, and set his feet on the floor.

Padding across the room, he snuck into the doorway to the kitchen. He hadn't been spotted so he took a few moments to enjoy the scene in front of him. The triplets were gobbling up French toast, having liberally saturated their slices with syrup. Shannon stood at the stove, wearing a short pink terry robe. She'd scrubbed her face shiny and, he was happy to see, her color had returned to normal.

"Wow, looks good enough to eat." Dean wiggled his brows when Shannon turned to stare, mouth agape.

She gestured at the last empty chair at the table and waved him toward it, brandishing her spatula.

"Go. Sit. How do you like your bacon?" The look she sent him suggested he not answer with a sexual innuendo this time.

"Crispy please. I take it you're feeling better?"

"Like a new person. It's amazing how fast you can get over something when you take the time to sleep it off." She kept her gaze focused on the frying pan, tiny dots of color staining her cheeks.

"Isn't it just?"

Dean ruffled Brian's hair, pointed to something on Brenna's plate, and stole a piece of bacon off the little boys' plate. Then he headed for the coffee pot, stopping to snag the creamer out of the fridge. The only thing that would make this morning better is if he were allowed to give in to the urge to take Shannon in his arms and kiss her. But he knew she wasn't ready for that.

He stirred a packet of sweetener into his steaming mug and glanced toward the table. The kids would be totally okay with him dating their mom. He had no doubt. They were old enough to understand that their mother deserved to be happy too. And when they were all together, they were happy. Just like a family.

"Earth to Dean? Bacon's ready." He blinked, realizing Shannon held a plate to his chest.

"I... thanks." He ignored her quizzical gaze and joined the kids at the table, replacing the bacon he'd stolen from Brian with one of his own.

The kids finished their breakfasts, downed their milk, and carried plates and glasses to the sink. Shannon slid into one of the vacated seats. She forked a stack of French toast onto Dean's plate, keeping only one for herself.

"I guess we need to get another chair for the table." She handed the syrup to Dean as though she'd just made a casual comment about the weather.

"Yeah?" As happy as this made him, he wasn't at all sure what to say.

"You saved my butt yesterday. I owe you big time." She cut her toast into tiny pieces.

"You don't owe me a thing. I was happy to help. If our roles were reversed, you would have taken care of me in a second." He took a big bite of maple-y goodness. "I know it's hard for you to accept help from someone, but you need to understand something. You aren't beholden to me, or anyone else. You can't always go it alone. Some days you are just going to have to admit you need help. And I hope you know that you can always come to me."

Shannon plucked a sliver of food into her mouth and chewed it thoroughly. She took a sip of milk. Finally she set her fork down and looked up at Dean. She nodded.

"I do know that. It blows me away, if you want the honest truth. But I do believe you."

They finished the rest of their breakfasts in companionable silence. Shannon stood up to clear the table so Dean took that moment to beat her to the sink. He filled the sink with hot, soapy water and took the breakfast dishes from her when she got there.

"I've got this. Why don't you grab a cup of coffee and have a seat?"

"Oh, no, my stomach isn't ready for coffee. I think I could go for some tea though." Shannon seemed pleased to be offered a chance to sit and relax.

He washed the dishes quickly, and moved on to the counters while the frying pan and skillet were soaking. Shannon sat at the table, still looking a little worn. Dean swept the sponge across the tabletop and paused to lay the back of his hand against her forehead. Nice and cool. She looked up and smiled, clasping his hand in one of her own.

Sparing the quickest of glances toward the doorway and finding it free of pint-sized spies, he leaned down and kissed her gently. She craned her neck and returned his kiss. Unspoken agreement kept it short and sweet. She fanned a hand in front of her face.

"Whew! There is nothing sexier than watching a man clean my kitchen. You're lucky I've got three little chaperones wandering around here somewhere."

Dean laughed. Feeling wicked, he turned back to the stovetop, presenting his backside, and pretended to scrub in slow, sensuous movements. She whistled, suggesting she needed to go search her purse for a stack of ones.

Once the kitchen was cleaned up, and a fresh cup of coffee poured, Dean and Shannon took their drinks out to her little patio. Several out-of-state cars were parked in the driveway of the big house. Dean hoped nothing would be asked of Shannon today. She still needed a day to get her strength back.

The triplets, realizing the party had been moved outdoors, raced out to their play structure. Shannon pulled demurely on the hem of her robe, probably only now noticing her state of dress. Personally, Dean hoped she'd stay in it all day.

"So I feel like I lost a whole day. What did you all do while I was sleeping?"

Dean filled her in on the adventures he and the kids had shared yesterday. They'd played pirates on the play structure. The boys had shown him the best rocks to look under for all sorts of creepy crawlers. Brenna had invited him to a tea party, insisting he wear one of her feather boas and a floppy hat, when she found that he didn't have anything formal to wear to the occasion.

"Oh, I would have loved a picture of that!"

"Any and all photos would have been confiscated and destroyed," he rumbled.

Then for dinner they had snuck up to the big house and made a fire in the fire pit. Dean sharpened sticks for everyone and showed them how to roast hot dogs over an open fire. Then they had made s'mores, and gotten covered in chocolate and sticky gooiness. After a bath that probably contained more bubbles than actual water, he read three books each and tucked them in.

"Mister, you were conned. They get *one* book each." Shannon chuckled.

"I had a feeling that was the case. But I was having too much fun to be the bad guy. It was a special occasion."

He reached out and covered Shannon's hand, shaking his head and silencing what would surely be either an apology or more undue gratitude. Brenna bounced up to them and slid into her mother's lap.

"Hey, baby girl. What's Rosie up to? I haven't seen her around lately." Shannon gave her daughter a squeeze.

"Silly Mommy. Rosie left. She went on the plane with Gramma."

"Is she visiting with Gramma for a while then?"

"No, she's exploring. She wants to see lots of places." Brenna kissed her mother on the cheek, wiggled out of her lap, and gave Dean a kiss as well, before darting off.

Shannon stared after her, her eyes misty. She sighed, but he couldn't tell if she was really happy or really sad. Something significant had just happened and he wasn't quite sure what it was.

"What am I missing? Her imaginary friend went away?"

"She doesn't need her anymore." Shannon looked up, smiling in spite of her trembling lower lip. "I would say you had a lot to do with that."

Dean felt a quick jab to the heart that slowly began to warm and spread. This family meant the world to him. He felt possessive. They were no longer the single mother and her children who lived next door. They were his. His Shannon ... his kids to help watch out for, care for.

Shannon had turned her attention back to the triplets. They were running and goofing off on the lawn. She clapped at their antics, looking like the happiest mom in the world.

He needed to tell her the truth. He had to trust that she wouldn't hate him for holding out on her. He had to trust that she wouldn't change on him once she learned that he came with a very colorful past. He owed it to her to be honest, finally. He just hoped it wasn't too late.

CHAPTER NINETEEN

Just go in! Shannon took another sip of her iced coffee as she made another pass in front of the dress shop that she had never been inside before. She normally bought her clothes at Wal-Mart, occasionally finding something on clearance at the mall. But these high end stores in the harbor were out of her comfort zone, not to mention her price range. Being the height of tourist season, she stood about as much chance of finding a clearance rack as she would finding enough snow in her yard to build a snowman.

Taking a deep breath, she tossed her drink into the garbage bin outside and pulled open the door to the boutique. The change in temperature was shocking, the air conditioning raising goose bumps on her bare arms. Shannon adjusted the strap of her purse and forced a small smile for the saleswoman behind the counter.

"Can I help you find anything?"

"I'm not exactly sure what I'm looking for yet. I'll let you know if I need any help."

She wandered to the back, knowing that was where most stores kept their cheaper items. As she'd expected, the racks were devoid of sale signs. Given that the vast majority of sales for the year, around here, were made during the three months of summer, she couldn't blame them. Folks who actually lived in Scallop Shores just didn't have the income to spend on fancy clothes. Businesses like this boutique counted on the fat wallets of vacationing tourists from Boston and New York.

Talia had told her about this place. She'd all but pushed Shannon out the door when she had dropped the triplets off. They were making homemade pizzas with Talia's twins and were eager to see their mom off with quick kisses and perfunctory hugs.

"He said he has something important to talk to you about. And it couldn't be discussed at a nice sit down restaurant? That means he expects sex after."

"Talia! You don't know that. He's shy, intensely shy, out in public. I'm not quite sure what's going on with that. I never did figure it out. I'm sure he just wants to talk in a place where he's comfortable."

"And if he asks you to take off all your clothes and get horizontal? Are you going to tell him no thank you?"

"Well, that wouldn't be a very polite way to treat my host, now, would it?" Shannon grinned.

"That's my girl!"

Clearly, she should have kept their one evening together to herself. Talia was such a hound. Shannon shook her head. She gave her friend a hug and headed for her car.

"If you decide to spend the night, text me. We'll bring the kids by in the morning."

Shannon waved her off, honking as she backed out of the driveway.

Now here she was, last minute shopping for a knockout dress that might, or might not, be for a booty call. To say she was nervous was putting it very mildly. Dean had promised steak and salad, so he did intend to have them eat. It wasn't just about the sex.

Shannon pulled a deep purple cocktail dress off the rack and held it against her. On anyone else it would look gorgeous. But with her shade of red hair, it just clashed. Her color palettes had always been so limited. It made shopping for clothes a lot less fun. Then again, given her budget, that was probably a good thing. She put it back and checked to see if they had a similar one in teal or emerald.

No, but she found a cute little spaghetti-strapped number in the most beautiful sapphire blue. The attraction was so immediate that she almost couldn't bear to check the tag. Anything she wanted this badly had to come at a price—a big price. Resigned to give up this newly coveted treasure, Shannon frowned, snatching at the tag and turning it to face her.

Okay, it wasn't cheap, but it wasn't totally unreasonable either. If she ended up getting the job as teacher's assistant, she'd have a second income starting in the fall. She could put it on a credit card and have it paid off by Christmas. Oh, who was she kidding? She'd justify it no matter what.

Holding her prize to her chest, she strode confidently to the register. The saleswoman complimented her choice, remarking on how closely the color in the dress matched her eyes.

"Special occasion?"

"Just a date, really."

"You're getting awfully dressed up for just a date. He must be someone very special."

"Yes, he's very special." Shannon handed over her credit card and shifted impatiently for her turn to sign the receipt.

"Have a wonderful evening. Maybe you'll be in soon to shop for a honeymoon trousseau?" Shannon blinked as the saleswoman waved goodbye.

Good Lord! That wasn't what this was about, was it? They barely knew each other. Yes, they had a good thing going. He was wonderful with the children. He was loving and caring and helpful and generous, everything that she had no business expecting in her life anymore. But marriage?

Her nerves completely jangled, Shannon spun her thinking around in the opposite direction. Laying the dress over the back of the passenger seat, she made her way around to her side of the minivan. What if he thought things were moving too fast? Or he didn't feel the same way about her that she felt about him. He was going to tell her that they needed to go back to just being neighbors.

Shannon had herself in a tizzy when she finally pulled into her own driveway and carried her purchase up to the cottage. She was tempted to chicken out, tell Dean she was still feeling a little ill and ask for a rain check. Doing breathing exercises to get a grip on her panic, she started to get ready for their date.

At 7 o'clock sharp, Shannon stood on his doorstep, waiting for Dean to answer the doorbell. She smoothed down the skirt of her new dress for the hundredth time. Had she remembered to cut the tags out? Was her lipstick too dark? *Cool it, girl. This is just a date.*

The door opened and her senses were immediately assaulted. Dean wore slacks, the fit tight through his muscular thighs. She knew the view would be even better from behind. His silky shirt, too, was tight. All the better to accentuate those killer pecs. Oh, she was a lucky girl! Shannon sniffed the air and her smile was full of surprised delight.

"That smells incredible. You cooked for me?"

"Aw, come on, don't sound so surprised. You taught me how to use that broiler. And it's pretty hard to mess up a tossed salad." He held out a hand and pulled her into the foyer, not releasing her hand until he'd caressed every part of her body using only his eyes.

"Promise me you will wear that dress every single day, for the rest of your life."

The rough kiss that followed indicated that Dean had promises of his own of how he intended the evening to go. Shannon trailed behind him, her legs more than a little shaky.

They wandered through to the kitchen, the scent of perfectly seasoned meat making it very hard to keep from drooling. Dean still held her hand and squeezed it when he got to the dining room. Shannon gasped. She'd never noticed the formal dining room, and with the way Dean had set everything up she was amazed.

A centerpiece of deep red roses set off the pristine white in the lace tablecloth. Irish lace? It was incredible. The man could set a table, too. The china was fancier than anything she'd ever eaten off of. She bet the flatware was real silver. And there were cloth napkins with fancy napkin rings. Shannon stared hard at the table. There really was a lot she didn't know about her neighbor.

"Oh, I forgot the lighter for the candles."

The timer went off in the kitchen and Dean turned a conflicted glance to the doorway.

"I'll get it. You get those beautiful steaks out. Where do you keep the lighter?"

"It's in the top left hand drawer of my desk, in my office."

"Be back in a jiffy."

Shannon made her way back down the hall, past the library that she longed to lose herself in at some point, past the den with the fireplace where she and Dean had spent a glorious evening. His office was nearer the front of the house.

A huge cherry wood desk faced the doorway. The window behind it looked out on the arborvitae hedges that separated their yards. Shannon pushed the plush leather chair out of the way and pulled out the drawer on the left. The lighter wasn't immediately visible, so she pulled a sheaf of papers out and set them on the blotter.

Doing a double-take at the official stamp, she gave the top page a once over. If she could take back any moment in her life, this would be the one. If she could go back and unread the truth she'd just learned, she would. Anything was better than finding out that Dean had fathered a child and was denying child support, denying his flesh and blood.

"Did you find it?"

"You could say that."

Shannon knew the exact moment that Dean caught up with the situation. The color drained from his face and he looked like he was struggling for just the right words, only his tongue was too tangled to speak.

Her lungs burning from unshed tears she forced herself not to lose it in front of him. She held up the stack of papers with a shaky hand and asked, with an equally shaky tremor in her voice, "I only have one question. Is this the important thing you wanted to talk to me about tonight?"

He lowered his focus to the carpet, his eyes full of shame and regret. "I was actually saving that one. It's not what you think, Shannon."

"It's not a paternity suit?" She shot him a chilly stare.

"Well, yeah, it is. But this woman, she's just out for money."

"You know what? I totally get that. I've spent the last five years raising my three children alone, and if my pride had let me, and I'd known where Vince was, I probably would have been 'out for money,' too."

He sputtered something but her pulse was pounding so loudly in her ears that Shannon could no longer hear a word he was saying. She slapped the papers down on the desk, slammed the drawer shut, and ran from the room. When Dean reached out a hand to stop her she sidestepped to avoid the contact. She was halfway down the driveway when she finally succumbed to tears.

CHAPTER TWENTY

How the hell did *she* end up the bad guy? Shannon stood in the doorway to Brenna's room, being given the cold shoulder, the same reaction she'd come across moments before in the boys' room. They were not taking this well. Her "I'm serious this time—no one steps one foot on Mr. Dean's property without major consequences" speech was met with pouts, stomps, and lots of whining. Oh, if only she were allowed to indulge in a good tantrum herself.

When her whispered "love you" was answered with silence, she started glumly down the hall to the kitchen. It was for the best. Dean wasn't the man she thought she knew. But then the joke was on her. She really never knew who he was. Who treats a neighbor's triplets like they meant more to him than the world, but wouldn't claim and help support a child of their own? Someone with no heart, that's who.

Shannon yanked open the fridge and studied the contents. It was baking time. She took out the carton of eggs and tub of margarine, almost forgetting herself and slamming the eggs to the counter. He made her angrier still, for affecting her like this. *Get out of my head, you jerk! Get out of my heart.*

Taking a shaky breath, Shannon moved to the pantry, gripping the door tightly as she searched for more ingredients to throw together. A single tear tracked down her cheek and she dashed it away with an angry swipe. *No, he's not worth this. He doesn't deserve to be cried over.* How many tearful nights had the mother of his child spent worrying over how she was going to afford to raise her baby?

Brownies or banana bread? Both. She'd have made something else too, if she'd had anything left in the pantry. It was time for a Costco run. Shannon emerged from the pantry, a box in each hand. She bumped the door shut with her butt. Sniffling, she dropped them off on the counter and dropped to her knees to dig out the hand mixer.

She measured out the ingredients for the brownies and turned the mixer on low, hoping she wasn't bothering her little sleepers. Her eyes burned with unshed tears, her chest ached. She wanted to howl, to just belt out a scream so loud it would wake the dead. Her head and her heart were at war over the infuriating man next door. Her head was telling her how foolish she was to let a man into her life, her heart. Men couldn't be trusted. They couldn't be relied upon.

But this one can, her heart cried. *This one is special.*

She hadn't given him a chance to explain. She frowned, pouring the smooth batter into the non-stick pan, her back straightening just a little. There again, her head and heart were in disagreement. Her head was claiming there was nothing that explained this beyond lack of character. Her heart tried to tell her that the man she knew would not abandon a child, any child, without good reason. Did he have a good reason?

The brownie pan went into the oven, the timer set and the bowl washed out for the banana bread. Shannon used a wooden spoon this time, stirring for all she was worth and hoping she didn't snap the spoon in her distress. She'd done that the night she'd baked after learning about her mother's upcoming nuptials. Wooden utensils probably weren't the best implements for a stress baker like herself.

Shannon set the bread pan on the counter to wait its turn in the oven. She briefly considered taking a glass of wine in for a good soak (and a cry, if she were being truthful) in the tub, but worried she wouldn't hear the timer. She poured the wine and carried the glass to her little roll top desk and her laptop.

She sank into the computer chair and took a large swallow of cabernet. What sucked, what really sucked, was that Dean was the one she had come to lean on during these moments when she just needed to talk, needed to cry … just needed someone. Who did she talk to when what she needed to talk about was him? And why, damn it, was he still the very first person she thought of?

Shannon groaned, setting her glass down and rubbing her aching temples with her fingertips. She still needed to explain things to Talia. Poor woman. She'd burst in like a madwoman to get the kids the night before, saying only that she'd talk to her later. Talia had called today. Dean had called too. She'd taken the phone off the hook. She wasn't accepting phone calls today. The kids were calling her "Mean Mommy."

Maybe her mom was on Skype. It wasn't their usual night, but that didn't mean she couldn't be online and surfing, shopping, or whatever it was women with actual free time did on the internet. Shannon took another slug of wine and opened up her browser. She had mail. The next sip of wine went down the wrong way and left her in a fit of coughing when she saw who the email was from. Vince Bainbridge.

Her fingers hovered over the keys. The urge to delete the email without reading it was almost impossible to ignore. Her heart and head were in agreement on this one: "Threat, threat!" They screamed as one. She stared at the screen, working up the courage to open the email. Shaky fingers scrabbled for the wine glass and she drained the contents. Here goes nothing.

Shannon,
The internet is a pretty small world. It was easier to find your email than I thought it would be.

I know this is too little too late, but I owe you all kinds of apologies. I was an immature kid who had no business getting married and bringing children into the world when I was too selfish to even take care of myself. Yeah, I know you sacrificed your own college career to become my wife and take care of me. And I thanked you by walking out when you needed me most.

Dad called me the other night. Said he saw the triplets. Said you've got a new guy. Told me to get my ass home. He's right. I need to come home. I need to own up to my mistakes. I want to meet my kids. I want to say sorry—in person. It's time, Shannon. I'm in upstate New York and plan to drive up for a quick visit. I'll be there in a few days. I can't wait to see you again.

Your reformed-deadbeat-ex-husband, Vince.

Shannon slammed the cover of her laptop, snatched a pillow off the couch, and ran out to the porch. Throwing herself full out on the porch glider, she stuffed her face in the pillow and screamed until her throat was raw and every ounce of emotion drained from her body. Then she went back inside to eat her way through a pan of brownies while her banana bread baked.

CHAPTER TWENTY-ONE

She wasn't taking his calls. He knew better than to show up on her doorstep. How was he supposed to fix this? Dean drove past Shannon's driveway on the way to his interview at the elementary school. She wasn't home. If he'd had flowers, he could have left them for her to find. She'd probably throw them away.

This was supposed to have been an exciting day for him. Shannon was supposed to know who he was by now. Then if he got the position as music teacher at Scallop Shores Elementary, they would have celebrated together. It was his chance to make a place for himself in the community.

Now he was starting to wonder if this was the place for him. In the short few months he'd been here, Scallop Shores had grown on him. He could separate out the locals from the tourists. He was starting to be recognized around town, not for his role as a former boy band member but as the newest addition to the town. It felt good. It felt right. But what if Shannon had let word spread about the paternity suit?

He wasn't giving her enough credit. But he couldn't help that small niggle of doubt, that stinging wound left by every other woman he'd dated. He knew he should trust her to keep his business private, and it disgusted him that he even let those doubts in. Shannon was different. He trusted her with his heart; now he needed to trust her with everything else.

"Hey, Dean." One of the local cops, Chase, if he recalled correctly, waved as he stepped out of Logan's Bakery.

Dean studied his face for censure and, finding none, smiled and waved back. He ducked into the shop and headed for the register to place his order.

"Good morning, Dean. How are things?" The woman who ran the joint, Cady, asked him.

"Great, just great. Can I get a latte to go?" He stared hungrily into the display case. "And a bear claw, please?"

"You got it." She started the milk steaming and then reached into the case for his pastry. "Where are Shannon and the kids today?"

Small town, indeed. "I, uh … " *How much to reveal?* "Shannon's not talking to me. I think I screwed this up."

"Oh, don't be silly. Whatever it is, she'll get over it."

"How can you be so certain?" Dean peeled off a few ones and handed them to Cady. She tried to drop the change in his palm but he pushed her hand toward the tip jar she kept on the counter.

"Shannon Fitzgerald making time with a man? Huge news, right there. When she came back to town to have those babies, she wouldn't have anything to do with anyone that owned a penis." A grizzled old man at the counter offered this sage advice.

"Mr. Feeney, that's TMI." Cady tsked.

"Don't know what TMI is, but that's the dang truth, that is. She even made sure she had a lady doc deliver those triplets."

"Aren't you glad you moved to this busybody town full of people who can't mind their own business?" Cady threw the question out to Dean while her scowl remained focused on Mr. Feeney.

"Actually, yeah I am. Call me crazy, but I'm really liking it here." Dean grinned, raising his latte in salute.

"Crazy! Just kidding. Listen, you got Shannon to open up to you. That's so huge. Give her some time and then see if she'll let you explain. Talk it out."

"Thanks."

"Hey, and good luck with the interview today."

Dean shook his head as he headed back out to his car. How the hell they learned some things and not others, it was just spooky.

•••

Shaking hands with the principal of Scallop Shores Elementary, Dean accepted the recently vacated position of music teacher. He had filled the man in on his background, finding it remarkably easy to talk about his past. Mr. Hobbs was excited with the energy and the experience that Dean would be bringing to his new role. He'd told him how lucky the children were to have him. Dean assured Mr. Hobbs that he was honored to be able to share his love of music with the students.

They agreed that it would probably be best to keep the boy band thing on the down low, just until everyone got to know him better. Even elementary-age children could get star struck and find it hard to focus on the learning, when what they really wanted to hear was what it was like to be a pop star.

Dean left the front office, started to head for the door, and turned at the last minute, deciding to do a little exploring of his new place of employment. The halls were empty, school still a few weeks away. He tried to imagine what it would be like when everyone returned: the noise, the laughter, the chaos. And he'd be a part of it. He couldn't wait.

He turned and headed down another vacant hallway. The walls were decorated with bright posters and handmade artwork. Kindergarten or first grade, perhaps? He was just passing a door with a huge construction paper apple tree, the apples blank and waiting for the names of the students who would attend that class, when the door opened, banging into his arm.

"Oh, my goodness! I am so sorry. Are you okay, sir?"

They both knew a moment of stunned silence when Shannon blinked in shocked recognition, withdrawing the hand that had reached out to rub his arm. Of all the people he expected to run into at the elementary school, she was definitely not one of them.

"Shannon, everything all right?" An older woman peered out of the classroom. "Sir? Are you a parent?"

"Hi, no I'm the new music teacher. Dean Patterson. Nice to meet you." He reached past Shannon to shake the teacher's hand.

"A pleasure. I heard Mrs. Dixon was retiring. I'm Wanda Peat. I teach first grade. Oh, and this is my new teacher's aide, Shannon Fitzgerald."

"We've met," Dean and Shannon mumbled simultaneously.

"Can I walk you to your car?" Dean asked Shannon, leaning down so only she could hear, "I have no idea how to get out of this place."

"I'll see you soon, Wanda." Shannon started off down the hallway and Dean hurried to keep up with her.

"Thanks. I got the crazy idea to do a little exploring and I got a lot lost." Dean tried to coax a smile from her and failed.

She looked at him sharply. "I parked in the faculty lot. That's where I'm headed. If you parked somewhere else, then you're on your own."

He jogged along beside her. "So teacher's aide, huh? Why didn't you tell me you'd applied for a job at the school?"

Dean winced, knowing he'd set himself up good with that one. Shannon gave him a cold stare but declined to take the bait. He let her walk a little ahead of him. He wasn't used to seeing her dressed up. Where Wanda had looked frumpy and matronly in her plaid skirt and clunky shoes, Shannon looked warm and approachable in a fuzzy short-sleeved sweater and flowery skirt that swished around her ankles as she walked. Her strappy white sandals showed off her tanned feet.

They had just reached the front door and had headed for the sidewalk when Shannon apparently couldn't contain her curiosity. She whirled around, her skirt showing a nice amount of calf before settling back down again.

"Music teacher? Where did that come from? And why did you have to pick *my* school? This was for me. I was finally doing something for me." She swiped an errant tear from her cheek and turned away again, hugging her arms tightly.

Aching to reach out, knowing he'd be rejected, Dean slapped at his empty pockets. Only dorks carried handkerchiefs. But at this moment he'd have loved to be that dork, the gentleman who's prepared for a woman's tears. Especially seeing as he was the cause of these tears. Shame and guilt crawled through his gut, leaving a burning trail in their wake.

"I have a background in music. I was looking for something, a way to contribute to the community, to give back. Something to keep me out of trouble." Nope, no smile that time either. "I didn't know you were looking into a job here too." He reached out a tentative hand and touched her shoulder. She didn't move. "This means more to you. It's such a big step for you. You know what? You deserve this. I shouldn't get in the way. I'll go back and tell them I can't take the job."

She turned around, eyeing him suspiciously. "You'd do that for me? Yours is a real job—the school music teacher. I'm just an aide. I'm not a real teacher; I just help out in the classroom."

"For the immediate future. But I bet you're also looking into college courses that you can take at home, online. Right? So you may be an aide right now, but someday you'll be a teacher. And you are going to affect the lives of so many people. You're the one they're going to be thanking as they stand up at the podium, giving their valedictorian speech on graduation day." This time she did laugh, though Dean guessed it was more from embarrassment than anything else.

"Shut up. I'm trying to stay away from you." She gave him a watery smile.

"You think I'm a bad person."

"I don't want to. But that *paperwork*," she spat the word out as though it tasted foul, "was pretty damning. You have to admit that."

"I admit it looked pretty bad. Would it sound cliché if I told you it wasn't what it seemed?"

"The truth, Dean. All I want is the truth. Is that so hard?"

He opened his mouth to speak. What did he have to lose at this point? Her face was upturned, expectant. His tongue wouldn't work. The words were frozen, just on the tip of his tongue. Dean stared miserably as Shannon sighed and turned away.

"It's not mine. The baby. You need to trust that it's not mine. I wouldn't fight this unless I knew 100 percent that I wasn't the father. Please believe me, Shannon."

"Whatever you say." Those strappy white sandals slapped against the cement as Shannon stalked off toward her car.

CHAPTER TWENTY-TWO

Dean checked his phone, made sure the conference call was working on all ends. "Toby, Jax, Linc, Gage? Everyone here?" They all answered in the affirmative.

"Guys, I'm calling in reinforcements. I need you here. This is big. Bring the wives, girlfriends, babies, and everyone that matters."

"Everyone that proves boy band members are capable of maintaining a real relationship?"

"Something like that." Dean sighed.

"Boys, I believe our lead singer has fallen in love," Gage pronounced.

"Dude, it's not too late. Run, run as fast as you can!"

"Shut up, Jax. You didn't tell her the truth yet, did you?" Toby admonished.

"I tried. I was planning on it, seriously. But she found the paperwork for that damned paternity suit before I could tell her." Dean scraped his free hand through his hair. "Now she thinks I'm this evil, deadbeat dad. I don't know … she probably thinks that's why I moved across the country. I messed up so bad."

"We'll make it right, Dino. But we do this for you and you owe us. You do the reunion show with us."

"I'll do it. Anything. I just want Shannon back."

"We'll be there as soon as we can get away. Don't do anything stupid … okay, stupider, until we get there."

"Hey, guys? Thanks for this. I really miss you all. It wasn't you I was running from. You know that, right? Just … the life. I was just sick of it."

"Ah, hell, he's getting mushy. I'm outta here. Later." Dean rolled his eyes as Jax dropped out of the conference call.

"We're looking forward to meeting Shannon and the kids. See you soon, Dino."

Dean said goodbye to the rest of the band and pressed "end call." Was he doing the right thing? He hadn't told her the truth when he should have. But maybe if he showed her his other life, in person … He hoped like hell that she'd understand the secrecy, the reasons it was so difficult to tell her the truth. Then he'd work on the truth behind the paternity suit. He hadn't lied about that.

• • •

Shannon stood up on shaky legs and went to the sink to rinse out her mouth. Nothing like a raging case of nerves to chase the food right out of her stomach. She grabbed a toothbrush and scrubbed her teeth and tongue. Studying her reflection, she groaned.

Vince had emailed last night to say that he was in town. He was staying with his parents. Given how his father felt about Shannon, he'd suggested they find a neutral place to meet. He left it up to her whether she wanted to include the children in this first meeting. The mama bear in her wanted to take her triplets and hide away with them, but in the end, she didn't have a choice. Talia was taking her boys for a check-up at the doctor. She didn't feel comfortable enough to foist all three kids on anyone else. She had to take them with her.

Dean would have been happy to watch them. But she couldn't go there, as much as she still longed to reach out to him, to tell him what was going on with Vince's visit. Dean would have insisted on going with her for moral support. Why did he have to be so damned perfect in nearly every way and so despicable when it came to family?

She brushed out her hair and let it fall loose around her shoulders. Vanity had her applying a light coat of makeup. Just because she was a single mom of triplets didn't mean she had to look dowdy. And she wasn't doing this for Vince's benefit. She couldn't care less what he thought of her. Though if she looked her best, and he just happened to have regrets, so much the better. Shannon stuck her tongue out at the mirror.

"Mommy, who are we meeting again?" Brian asked as they were piling into the minivan.

"Vince is an old friend of Mommy's, from before you were born. He doesn't live in Scallop Shores anymore." And hopefully wouldn't be moving back, either.

"Careful! You almost squished Rosie, Mommy." Brenna patted a tiny spot next to her in her booster seat.

"Ah, is she back from her travels, then?"

"Yeah, she was lonely and asked if she could come live with us again."

Shannon ducked her head as she finished fastening seat belts. Hot tears pricked her eyelids. This was her fault. She was screwing up her daughter's life by taking away the one person, outside their immediate family, that she had come to love so much. And now she was introducing her to the man who failed her before she'd even been born? Her mother-of-the-year rank was sinking lower by the minute.

"If we go with you to meet your friend, then can we go visit our friend later?" Brady asked hopefully.

"Sure. Who would you like to visit?"

"Mr. Dean. We haven't seen him in a long time and he must be really sad about that. It's been too long, Mommy."

Twist the knife a little deeper, my sweet boy. Shannon didn't reply, didn't think she could, without crying. She started up the van and headed for the tide pools at the harbor.

He stood beside his car, a Mini Cooper. Well, he certainly hadn't come equipped to safely transport his children anywhere. If Shannon had been hoping Vince had lost his looks to balding and paunch, she was disappointed. He was still just as dreamy as he'd been in high school and college, a little more filled out, hair a little neater.

"I told them you're an old friend of mine from high school. They don't know any more than that," she muttered through her teeth, once she had gotten out and stood beside him.

"I've missed you too, babe." Shannon stood still, arms stiff at her sides, as Vince leaned down to hug her.

"We're on the same page? I turn around and go if you aren't."

"I'll be on my best behavior. I swear." He held his hands palms up.

With a curt nod, Shannon turned and slid open the door to the minivan. The children had already unbuckled themselves and stood blinking owlishly at their mother's "friend." She stepped out of the way and let them jump down on their own. No one said a word as they stood in the parking lot, scuffing their sneakers and sending covert glances toward the stranger.

"Brenna, Brian and Brady, this is Mommy's old friend, Vince. Vince, these are my children." Her steely gaze dared him to challenge her right to parent them on her own.

"Hey, why don't you all go see what there is to discover in the tide pools today? Brian, no putting baby crabs in your sister's hair, got it?"

The children dashed off, old enough to pick up on uncomfortable vibes and eager to remove themselves from the situation. Shannon and Vince followed them down to the beach. She found a bench, close enough to keep an eye on the kids but far enough away so they couldn't overhear the conversation. Vince sat down beside her and she automatically scooted a few inches away.

"They're beautiful. And so happy." Vince stared after the children, his expression dazed.

"And they are well-behaved five-year-olds. Just because there are three of them doesn't mean that they are out of control hooligans."

Her heart squeezed as she recalled that awkward introduction to Dean.

"I can see that. You are a great mom. I knew you would be."

"You thought, at one point, that you'd be a good father. Until you learned you'd made three babies at once." Tension had her fingernails digging painfully into her thighs. "Did your fathering skills suddenly kick in? Why now? Why are you here?"

Vince took his eyes off the kids and focused his attention on Shannon. He looked tired, drawn. She straightened her spine, set her jaw rigid. As far as she was concerned, Vince was the enemy.

"I made so many mistakes when I was younger. I was selfish. I didn't want to give up the lifestyle I had."

"You mean the one where your wife paid for you to go to school and live in an apartment and not have to work?" She looked down her nose at him.

"I treated you horribly. And then I took my dad up on his offer to pay for the rest of my schooling, if I'd just leave you and the babies. He got me into a school in upstate New York. He paid for it all. But I was feeling so guilty about it, not telling you, taking his money, that I shut my parents out of my life too. I was their only son. My mom was devastated. Dad, too, I guess."

"You weren't freaked out about the babies? You just wanted to leave?"

"I wanted my career. I put my career plans first." He put his face in his hands.

"And how is that going, by the way? You must be in medical school now, right? What's your focus? I mean, it's gotta be big, right? You gave up a lot to be a big time doctor. You going to be a brain surgeon?" She'd been going for snide, snotty. Apparently, it didn't come out like the verbal slap it had been intended.

"Actually, I'm going into pediatrics." Vince looked animated for the first time since they'd sat down.

"Unbelievable." Shannon pinched the bridge of her nose and fought the tension headache that was starting to throb behind her right eyelid.

"I'm paying back my father, a little at a time. I want to start paying child support too."

"You aren't making the big bucks yet, Vince. How are you able to pay child support?"

"I eat a lot of boxed mac and cheese and ramen noodles. Food at the cafeteria is cheap, and I practically live there, so ... "

"We don't need your money. We've done just fine without you."

"My mom would like to meet the triplets. She's been wanting to so bad." Vince turned to face Shannon, his face scrunched into a grimace. "My dad lied to her. He said you kicked me out. He told her you didn't want the Bainbridges anywhere near your babies."

"Why would he do that? I could have used the help when I first brought them home. They could have used someone else to love them, care for them." A tear slipped down her cheek.

"He needed someone to blame. It should have been me, Shan. I'm so sorry. He was just so angry that I cut them out of my life. He took it out on you. It's all my fault."

"He wants you to take them from me, doesn't he? He wants me miserable and he knows if he asks, you'll fight me for custody and win."

"I won't lie. Yeah, he wants me to fight for custody. But I have no intention of doing it." He pressed a tissue into her hand and stared hard. "You've raised these kids. You are an amazing mom. They are blessed. Changing that, taking you out of the equation, would be the worst thing we could possibly do to them."

"Why are you here, then? If you don't want to take the kids from me, why are you here?"

"I've met someone. She's a lab technician at the hospital." Vince turned his head, staring off at the horizon. "We're getting married."

Warning bells clanged in her head. He may say he wasn't going to take the kids, but he had a more stable living environment for them than she did. Shannon's heart raced and her breathing became so shallow she thought she'd faint.

"She wants my babies. What is it? She can't have kids and you're going to give her mine?"

"Listen to me, you aren't being rational. I came here to make amends, so I can move on with my life." Vince took Shannon's hands in his own, holding firmly when she tried to snatch them away. "I haven't told Claire about being married before. She doesn't know I have kids. I want to tell her the truth. I want this thing I have with her to work. I'm done being a screw up, Shan. I've changed."

"What are you going to tell your father?" This time she did manage to tug her hands free. She stood up and put the wooden bench between them.

"I told him about Claire. I said there will be more babies. Maybe not for a while, but when we're ready. He and Mom will be a part of my life, of my children's lives from this point on. But these three? They are yours."

"Damn straight they are!" Shannon couldn't quite keep the quaver from her voice.

"Would it be okay if I got to know them a little, before I go? I swear I'll never let on that I'm their real father."

Shannon nodded mutely and he continued.

"Dad said you've got a boyfriend, some guy new to town. He said he's real good with the kids, treats them like his own. I'd say they're pretty lucky to have him. Dad, being Dad, said I should have words with him. Let him know who their real father is. Rough him up if I need to get my point across."

"God, that man is such a jerk! I hate to speak ill of anyone, really, but your father has no redeeming qualities whatsoever."

Shannon spat the words out, rolling her eyes while her nostrils flared. She fisted her hands at her sides.

"So aren't you glad you have no ties to my family anymore?" He grinned, shrugging his shoulders.

If she could only shrug it off as easy. Hollis Bainbridge was a horribly unpleasant man who was starting to make her very nervous. This meeting with Vince hadn't turned out as badly as she'd anticipated, but now Shannon was on edge. She didn't trust the older Bainbridge not to do something to ensure he got his way.

CHAPTER TWENTY-THREE

Another year older, another year wiser? Shannon slathered frosting on the last cupcake and stood back to assess her work. Shaking her head, she licked the extra frosting from the knife, deciding she wasn't quite done. Sprinkles—pink ones! It was her birthday, after all. She found the pink sugar crystals on her spice rack and gave each cupcake a little facelift.

The kids had been hounding her to invite Dean to her birthday barbeque the following afternoon. It was getting harder and harder to say no. "Mean Mommy" was no longer a way to stick it to her—it had become her permanent new name. Shannon was sick of being punished for keeping them apart. Maybe it was time to stop running away and give him a chance to explain himself. If he finally would.

Besides, if she were being completely honest with herself, she missed him. It chafed to have to admit that. It had been a long two weeks since she'd stormed out of Dean's house after discovering that sickening lawsuit.

She wasn't excusing his choice to deny his poor child in that awful paternity suit. She'd never excuse that. But everyone made bad choices at some point in their lives, right? Ugh. Having Vince pop back into her life in as positive a manner as could ever be hoped for had turned Shannon into a big softie.

For old times' sake she had even invited him to her birthday. This time last year she would have never conceived of reconciling with Vince on any level. Or falling in love with another man. Okay, so she was a long way from ironing out her issues with Dean, but she was also worlds away from the woman who had sworn off men forever.

Throwing all the dirty bowls and utensils into a sudsy dish pan, Shannon turned her back on the mess. It could wait a few minutes. She'd jot a quick note to Dean, invite him to the party, and slip it under his door. It was up to him whether he joined them for the celebration. She could extend an olive branch ... from a safe distance.

She checked on the kids one last time, each one snuggled up with a favorite stuffed animal, fast asleep. She scribbled an invite to Dean and slipped out the front door, locking it behind her. Then she headed for the part in the hedge.

Dean's house was all lit up, music coming from the big deck along the side. Curious, she crossed the dew-covered lawn in bare feet, the cool condensation tickling her toes. She stood in shadow, the lights on the side of the house cozily encircling the deck.

A group of people were talking and hanging out up there. Beer bottles clinked and potato chip bags rustled. Shannon detected the spicy tang of Polly's Pizzeria pizza. She'd recognize that scent anywhere. *Oh, Dean. You entertain a house full of people and* still *order pizza?* Had she taught him nothing about cooking?

"Hey there, big guy. You are growing up so fast."

Shannon narrowed her gaze on Dean, who was holding a baby in his arms, nuzzling him and tickling his little belly. Her heart squeezed as she took in the sight. He was a natural. Clearly, he knew the little cherub and doted on him like a favorite uncle. She frowned in consternation. Why was he so loving and generous of his affection for other people's kids, but not his own? What was she missing here?

Frustrated, confused, and more than a little jealous to be left out of this impromptu party, Shannon skulked back the way she'd come. The note she'd intended to slip under Dean's front door was forgotten, crushed in her fist. She felt another sweet pang when his laughter rang out across the lawn. She hurried as fast as her unshod feet would take her back to the cottage.

• • •

"Dude, there is some kind of party going on over there. Should we wait until it's over?" Jax had wandered into the kitchen, hands shoved into the back pockets of his cut off denims.

"I've waited too long as it is. I say we crash it."

"Rock on!"

Dean went to the counter and lifted the heavy crystal vase containing a dozen red roses. Women were suckers for roses, right? If she took the news of his previous life well, these would be the icing on the cake. Or maybe they'd be the consolation prize? He set the vase back down, wiped his sweaty palms on his khaki shorts, took a deep breath, and picked the flowers back up.

"You'll do fine. She's not going to throw a scene in front of a yard full of guests." Toby patted him on the back.

"Okay, but what if she sees my bringing you guys into it as cashing in on my celebrity status?"

"The Shannon you described to us would see it as you bringing your closest friends, those who understand you and the decisions you've made that brought you out here, to help explain your unique situation."

Dean started to speak and abruptly shut his mouth. Toby made a very good point—it was time to put his faith in Shannon. He looked around the kitchen at the considerably large group of people who had traveled all the way across the country just to lend moral support so he could spill his guts to the woman who held his heart.

"Hey, I just want to thank all of you."

"Yeah, yeah, let's go crash the party, Mush Man." Jax threw a wicked grin over his shoulder as he loped out of the kitchen and down the hall to the front door.

Given the social gathering taking place next door, and the size of the group about to drop in, Dean led them down the driveway and around to Shannon's cottage—not through the space in the hedge and onto the middle of her lawn. There were pink balloons tied to weights and sitting in bunches around the yard. People milled around, balancing paper plates and plastic cups.

Shannon stood supervising the blow up kiddie pool. A tall, lean man with auburn hair and laughing eyes stood beside her, his gaze intent on the three redheads screeching in the water. He leaned in close when she started to tell him something. Dean's breath caught in his throat, the sucker punch to his gut causing his head to reel. He knew who that guy was without being introduced.

No wonder he hadn't been invited to this shindig. Her ex was back in town. Maybe that's what this party was all about. A "happy to have you back in our lives" party. He wrinkled his brow. That just didn't jive. But since he hadn't been so great at opening up, he had no right to expect that she'd laid all her cards out. Could be she'd secretly hoped for this reunion ever since Vince left.

"Oh, my gosh! Five of Hearts! Shannon, it's Five of Hearts!" Shannon's friend, Talia, had spotted the group and was running toward them, while gesturing for Shannon to do the same.

"Showtime." Dean took a deep breath and put on his biggest smile.

"It was killing me—I knew I knew you from somewhere. But you weren't exactly forthcoming. Dino Valentine of Five of Hearts." She continued babbling but Dean picked up on one sentence in particular: "What a great birthday present!"

"Ah, crap, it's her birthday?"

"You didn't know? What are the roses for then?" Talia shook her head, obviously disgusted with herself for not having figured it out earlier. "You're here to get her to talk to you again."

"Looks like she's got another visitor too."

"Yeah, her ex. How weird is that?" Talia scrunched up her nose, shrugging her shoulders.

Shannon finally made her way across the lawn. She studied the group suspiciously, her eyes coming to rest on the vase of roses. She looked up at Dean. Her smile was hesitant. She looked nervous.

"Happy birthday," he said as he handed over the heavy vase.

"You didn't really know it was my birthday." It wasn't a question.

"Incredible timing?" She chose to ignore this.

"Who are your friends?"

Dean watched her expression. She was either a very good actress, or she honestly had no clue who they were.

Talia vibrated with latent teeny-bopper excitement. She was bouncing on the balls of her feet. She whipped her head around and gave her friend an incredulous look. "Are you serious? Five of Hearts? Hottest boy band in the country for a good five years?"

"Actually, we were even more popular in Japan, Australia, and the UK." Gage bowed deeply.

"Sorry, guys. No offense, but I didn't do boy bands. I was too busy working every spare chance I got from the time I was twelve, just to help my mom put food on the table."

Dean wanted to laugh at the absurdity of the situation. All this time, he had been trying to hide his identity from someone who wouldn't have known who he was if he'd jumped up on stage with the group and sung a ballad in her honor. Belatedly, he realized the fact that he'd had everyone fly out here to help explain the truth was a colossal waste of time and money. She wasn't going to understand.

"Hey, so before I get all fan girl on you guys, why don't I take you around and introduce you to the folks of our humble town." Talia pushed Dean toward Shannon, effectively separating him from the rest of the group.

"If everyone is as pretty as you, this is going to be a rockin' good time." Jax winked.

"Yeah. Let me start by introducing you to my husband and twin boys." She shot him a "don't even go there" look. The rest of the guys were howling at Jax's faux-pas.

Dean couldn't look at Shannon. His eyes traveled the crowd, landing on Vince, who was tossing marshmallows in the air and catching them in his mouth. The kids were following suit, but the lawn was littered with their failed attempts.

"More than one surprise guest today? Or did he get an invite?" Dean immediately felt like a heel when he saw her wince.

"I tried. But you were busy with your own party last night and I didn't want to intrude."

She was jealous! Maybe this meant he had a chance after all. Dean took her hand and led her away from the party. When they caught Vince's eye, Shannon tugged her hand away. Or maybe he was getting his hopes up for nothing.

"I've missed you. I called you. When you didn't answer ... or call me back, I figured stopping by would pretty much be considered stalking."

"The kids would have liked that. They have not been very happy with me lately."

Not "I've missed you too." The kids missed him. Well, that was okay, because he'd missed the heck out of them as well.

"So this was your big secret. You're in a boy band." She spoke slowly, like she was still trying to wrap her mind around it.

"Was—I was in a boy band. We went our separate ways about ten years ago. Toby is married. That's Vanessa with their son. Cute kid. Linc is married, with a baby on the way. Gage is getting married next month, on the Queen Mary. That's Tilly, his fiancée, in the green dress."

"And the one coming on to every woman here?"

"Yeah, that'd be Jax. He's still single. He gives us pop stars a bad name." Dean felt himself blushing.

"He was here before." She spoke the words so softly he almost missed them.

"I had a feeling you'd seen us that day at the beach."

"You didn't introduce me. I figured I just didn't rank up there."

"That wasn't it at all! I didn't want to introduce *him* to you. I was afraid once you saw the two of us together that you'd figure out who I really was."

"So Dean Patterson, the man who moved in next door last May, is just a façade? The 'real' you is someone else?" She tilted her head and gave him a probing stare.

"Well, no. I guess they're both me. I didn't change by moving out here." Dean stopped talking abruptly and blinked. "Wait. I'm not being honest here. I guess I really did change when I moved out here. I became this sneaky guy who was constantly trying to hide his past. I was so worried about you finding out who I was and turning into the type of woman I'd dated in the past, all greedy and fixated on fame, that I ended up someone that I don't even like." His voice trailed off and he met her sad gaze, his own apologetic.

"So when you said that you knew, one hundred percent, that you couldn't be that child's father … ?"

"It's part of the celebrity package. More money than you know what to do with. Girls hanging off your arm. Houses in Malibu. And people trying to figure out how to get themselves a piece of it."

"Was she a jealous ex-girlfriend?"

"I don't even know her—we've never met. My lawyer did some digging. Turns out she was in the background of a photo that made it to all the trashy rags out there. She was angled just well enough that it looked like we might have been together, a couple."

"And she was going to cash in on that? Take your money to raise her child?"

"Hey, at least this one actually had a child to pimp out. I was involved in a paternity suit once where the girl used photos and a birth certificate of a baby cousin. She'd never even given birth." He took the look of incredulous shock on her face as a good sign.

"I guess I shouldn't have judged you so quickly. I don't blame you for wanting to hide such ... nastiness." She slipped her hand into his, squeezing lightly. "Nail her to the wall, Dino!" Her eyes blazed as she grinned up at him.

Dean shook his head, cracking a smile at the possessive determination on Shannon's face. "Actually, when she realized we weren't going to settle easily, that we were going to take it all the way to trial, she dropped the suit."

They were quiet for a moment, staring into each other's eyes. His little world was finally getting back on track. He started to lean in for a stolen kiss.

"Hey, so this is the guy who has my kids wrapped around his little pinkie." Dean stood back in surprise as Vince loped forward and stuck his hand out for a shake.

"Dean, this is my ex-husband, Vince. Vince, this is Dean." A tense smile pasted to her face, Shannon looked like she wanted to be anywhere but there.

"How about those triplets? Aren't they the cutest dang things? It's like God took the best parts of Shannon and me and mixed them up into those little angels. They've got some great things to say about you. Why don't you go on over and say hi?" *So I can have Shannon all to myself again*, was what Dean heard.

He nodded, smiled sadly at Shannon, and walked away. He watched the kids playing with their friends. Brenna was even holding Toby's baby on her lap, Vanessa watching closely. If he had only realized their lives would have blended so seamlessly, he wouldn't have hesitated to tell Shannon the truth.

But now it was too late. Vince was staking his claim. He had come back to Scallop Shores, back to his family. Dean may not agree that Vince was the best father for those kids—in his heart, he knew the best man for that job was him—but Vince had him beat with a biological tie that he could never top.

He ducked through the hedge before the triplets could see him. It would just be too painful for him to spend time with them, hold them, and laugh with them, when he knew their dad was back in the picture. The sounds of the party diminished as he walked across his own lawn, pausing to glance at the flowers growing riotously under the tree Brady had fallen from shortly after he had moved in. God, that seemed like a lifetime ago now.

He wondered how much longer they would live next door. Surely, Vince would be getting a place in town. He was going to miss the hell out of those kids. But missing Shannon just might kill him.

CHAPTER TWENTY-FOUR

Bright sunshine spilled through the parted bedroom curtains, a happy start to a happy day. Shannon rolled over and smiled at the roses she'd placed on the bedside table before turning in last night. She wanted them to be the first thing she saw, the first thing she smelled in the morning. The buds were just starting to open. So beautiful.

Sliding her legs out from under the sheets, she sat up and stretched. All was right with the world, her world. For the first time in her children's lives, she could envision a future that involved a complete family. Dean wasn't a deadbeat dad. He was a loving, compassionate man who cared for her children just as she did.

She couldn't wait to tell the kids that they had worked things out yesterday. They'd finally be done with "Mean Mommy." Maybe they could ask Dean and his friends, band mates (now *that* was going to take some getting used to), to the beach. It was perfect weather for it. Wait. Would they get mobbed by fans? Maybe they should pick someplace quieter? It didn't matter. She just wanted to spend time with him and get to know his friends.

Whistling, Shannon practically skipped down the hallway to the kitchen. When the triplets finally began stumbling from their rooms, she'd almost finished their happy face pancakes. She was confused when they didn't seem more enthused with the special breakfast treat.

"What's with the sour pusses this morning?"

"He didn't even say hi." Brian pouted.

"Why'd he leave so fast? You made him leave." Brady was downright mutinous.

"I don't understand. Mr. Dean and I had a nice talk."

"He doesn't love us anymore. You messed things up, Mommy." Brenna shoved her plate away and folded her tiny arms across her chest.

"I'm sure you all are just misunderstanding things. I made things all better at the party. Well, he did. It doesn't matter." Shannon wrinkled her brow, shaking her head. "I don't know why he didn't come over to say hi to you guys, but maybe he was just distracted."

"Call him. Call him and tell him we want to see him."

"I was planning on it." Shannon stopped just short of sticking her tongue out at her cheeky son's bossiness.

Snatching up the phone, she punched in Dean's cell number. She turned to see that three expectant faces were watching her closely. She smiled big, to make up for their dubious frowns. Dean answered on the second ring.

"Hey there. It's Shannon ... and the kids. We were hoping you and your friends could join us for something fun today. It's so beautiful out."

"Thanks, that's nice of you. But I don't think it's a good idea. I was just going to take everyone around for a little sightseeing."

"Um, yeah, of course. But who better to show them around than a native, right?"

"I just want to spend some time with them before they have to leave. Maybe we'll bump into you in town or something."

"If that's what you want, sure. Maybe we'll see you around."

"Shannon? I appreciate your calling, but I really think it's best if we keep our distance."

"But I thought we had cleared things up yesterday? I thought you missed us."

"I do miss you. I always will. But things definitely got cleared up. I've got to go. Enjoy that beautiful weather." The hum of the ended call was obnoxiously loud in her ear.

The kids had heard her end of the conversation and had gotten enough out of it to learn that they would not be seeing Dean that day. Chairs scraped against the linoleum as the army of three trooped out of the room. No one so much as looked at her.

Shannon began to clean up the breakfast dishes in a fog. What had that been about? He'd sounded so sad. She should have given him the chance to explain things that first night. She'd waited too long. But why had he come to tell her the truth, then, if it wasn't with the understanding that he wanted to pursue a relationship? Once again, she was left with the feeling that she was the odd man out, the only person who hadn't been given all the pieces to the puzzle.

• • •

Once again Dean found himself in the role of tour guide, though his heart really wasn't in it. He kept thinking back to his call from Shannon. Why *had* she called? It had been childish to give her the brush off like that. But seeing her, seeing the kids, and knowing they were all moving on with Vince, it was just too much.

Besides, she'd invited his friends to go with them. That meant she probably intended to bring Vince. The more the merrier, right? He'd had to shut that one down fast.

"You're just going to let her go that easy? I thought you had more balls than that." Jax, sitting in the front seat of the rented Suburban, shook his head.

"He's their dad, Jax. I can't compete with that."

"No, you can *top* that. The jerk left his pregnant wife to raise their triplets—not one, but three babies—by herself. She is much better off with you."

"Okay, ideally, yeah. But he's made this freak reappearance. I'm not sure why now, after all these years. But don't I owe it to her to let her figure things out in her head?"

"Hell, no! This is where you let him know she's already taken— Shannon and her kids. Too bad, so sad. He had his chance. Screw him!"

"I'm not really into the whole caveman routine, Jax." Dean grinned at his friend. "And I find it odd that the person giving me advice on getting the girl is the person who runs as fast and furious from a commitment as he can get."

"Well, yeah ... different strokes for different folks, ya know?" Jax coughed into his fist and feigned interest in something just outside his window.

Dean smiled. He'd really missed these guys. They'd all been through a lot together. Now marriage and kids. Well, for him it'd be the other way around. A ready-made family. Jax was right. He had to fight for what he knew was his. He was a better fit for Shannon and her triplets. She could count on him. He'd never leave.

As though thinking of her had magically conjured her presence, Dean spotted Shannon in the small dirt lot beside a local farmer's market. She was screaming and she looked absolutely terrified. The kids! He yanked the steering wheel, kicking up gravel, as he tore into the parking lot, threw the SUV into park, and yanked open his door.

"Hey, hey, I'm here, how can I help?" He gripped her shoulders and forced her to pay attention.

"I was picking out corn from the big cardboard bin. They were standing right beside the cart. I wasn't more than a few seconds. When I stood up, they were gone. All of them. My babies." Shannon was close to hyperventilating. Her head whipped back and forth and she searched the parking lot, her eyes brimming with tears.

"Okay, let's look around. They've got to be around here someplace. It's not that big." He started to head into the market.

"Dean, I've been looking for half an hour. They aren't here!" Shannon swiped at her tear-streaked face. "I think ... what if ..." Her voice trailed off and Dean felt a burning sensation deep in his gut.

"Hollis Bainbridge." His voice had turned deep, menacing.

Face white as a sheet, she nodded.

Dean ran to the SUV and filled everyone in. He told them to park and spread out, looking for the triplets. He suggested a few of the beach shops that he knew they loved and were within walking distance. He explained that he and Shannon had a lead and they were going to check it out.

Taking the keys from Shannon's trembling fingers, Dean led her to her minivan and helped her into the passenger seat. Running for the driver's seat, he gunned the engine and peeled out onto the road, waiting for her to lead him to the Bainbridge residence.

"Have you called Vince yet?"

"No. Why?" Shannon looked perplexed.

"He's their father. He'll want to know his children are missing." Dean tried to state the obvious as gently as possible.

"I'll fill him in after this is all over." Shannon pointed right when the road branched in two.

"Well, where is he? We can pick him up on the way."

"He left sometime last night. He's back home in upstate New York now." She sent an irritated look his way. "Why are you trying to involve Vince in this? He has his own life now. These are *my* kids that have gone missing. And if Hollis Bainbridge had something to do with it, Heaven only knows what I'll do to him."

Wait, so Shannon and Vince weren't reconciling? There was hope for him after all! A wildly inappropriate urge to let out a joyous whoop was only squelched by Dean's fear for the welfare of Shannon's children. He shared in her protective need to find them safe and sound. There would be time to celebrate later—as a family.

They pulled up to a white raised ranch on a side street in the center of town. The driveway was empty, but Dean could see a couple of vehicles in the attached garage. Someone was home.

Shannon hadn't even waited for the van to stop before she'd flung herself out the door, already running for the porch steps.

"Hollis Bainbridge, get your ass out here!"

"Shannon? What on earth has gotten into you?" An older woman stepped out the front door, hands on her wide hips. Could this be Eden Bainbridge, Hollis's wife and Vince's mother? She was looking at Shannon as though the young mother had lost her mind.

"Where is he, Eden? Where are my kids?" Shannon's voice was raw with unshed tears. Dean had managed to catch up to her and gripped her hand tightly, lending her his strength.

"Well, isn't this revealing? Give this woman a Mother of the Year award. She's managed to lose not one, but three kids. That's talent, folks." Hollis had appeared behind his wife.

"What did you do with them?" Shannon would have been in the man's face if it weren't for the restraining arm Dean flung around her waist.

"I don't have your kids, you crazy woman! Why would I take them?"

"Because you've threatened it. Because you wanted Vince to steal custody from me. Because you've told horrible lies to everyone you love just to ruin my life." Shannon was sobbing now.

Eden shot a glare over her shoulder as she reached for Shannon. The hate in her eyes told Dean this probably wasn't the first time the older man had played with his family's emotions. The younger woman collapsed in her arms. "Hollis, you have a lot of explaining to do once this is over." She straightened Shannon up, wiped the tears from her face, and hugged her hard. "Young lady, you go home and wait by the phone. If the police have any leads, they will call you there. Hollis and I will do anything we can."

Dean reached for Shannon's hand and drew her with him to the minivan. She kept looking back at the house, back at Hollis. He knew how she felt. It was their only lead and it hadn't panned out.

Now they truly had no idea where the triplets had gone. Doing as Mrs. Bainbridge had suggested, Dean headed for the cottage.

"I didn't even wait for the police to arrive at the Farmer's Market, Dean. They need pictures. I'm not doing this right." She looked lost, so young and so lost.

"We'll find them. We'll find them together." He reached for her hand and she grabbed it for the lifeline it was.

"I knew I could count on you, Dean. I knew it was safe to trust you with my heart, my kids. I love you so much. Don't ever leave."

She was babbling. Dean would give anything to know those words were true, but Shannon was under an incredible strain and probably wasn't even aware of what she was saying. When this was all over, and the kids were safely back home, he hoped to hear those words again.

• • •

A police car awaited them in the driveway. Did they have her children? Were they safe? Her throat was closed so tightly she couldn't even cry. Her stupid fingers wouldn't work on the door handle. She slapped ineffectually at the window. The door opened from the outside and Dean reached in for her, lifting her bodily from the car.

"Mommy!"

Shannon slid from his arms and looked around, desperately, for the source of that sweet little voice. A police officer had opened the door to the back of the cruiser and all three of her little angels were tumbling out. They met in a tangle of arms and bobbing red heads. She kissed every surface she could find, searching for injuries.

"Ms. Fitzgerald? I'm Officer Eaton. I found your children at the Farmer's Market down by the beach." He shook her hand and gestured to the kids. "I believe they have something to tell you."

Shannon sat down in the driveway, sobbing. She gathered everyone into her lap at once. Holding on so tightly, she had to remind herself to be careful not to hurt them. She closed her eyes, absorbing the warmth of their little bodies, the sweet smell of their hair. Her babies were home. They were safe. She could breathe again.

"We were bad, Mommy. You should punish us." Brady took the lead on this one.

"It was my idea. You said Mr. Dean was gonna be at the beach too. I thought we could go find him. We just wanted to see him again. Spend time with him." Brian held tightly to her neck and mumbled into her throat.

"But we aren't allowed to cross the street by ourselves. We got away from you and went out to the street and saw that we couldn't go anywhere." Brenna's eyes were huge, brimming with tears.

"Then you were running around and screaming. We were in a ton of trouble. We got scared."

"And so we hid from you. But then it got quiet. We came out of the back room and you were gone. Our van was gone. You left." Brady's lower lip was quivering as he looked to his mother for answers.

"Oh, baby, I thought someone took you. I thought I knew who did it and I rushed off like a fool to go take you back." Shannon stroked her son's hair, sending an apologetic look at the police officer, who had taken out a small notebook when he heard this.

"I should never have left the market. I didn't know." Shannon dropped another round of kisses on cheeks, elbows, and sweaty foreheads. Dean crouched down beside her.

"Your mom was doing what she thought was best. She loves you so much and you all gave her a very big scare."

"Mommy, Mr. Dean, we're so sorry. We didn't mean to scare you." They all hung their heads in shame.

Brenna sniffled, reaching out her hands so that she held one of her mother's and one of Dean's. "Do you still love us?"

Dean gathered the little girl into his own lap and reached for Shannon's free hand. He dropped a kiss onto Brenna's head and smiled at Shannon. "Yes, of course we still love you."

• • •

Shannon tucked the covers around one side of her big bed, while Dean did the other side. She left one of the bedside lamps on and joined him at the foot of the bed. He gathered her into his arms and they stood quietly for a moment, watching the triplets sleeping peacefully. Part of her wanted to stay there, ever vigilant. She knew today's scare would stay with her the rest of her life.

"Come on out here. I think today's adventures call for a nice glass of wine," he whispered, taking her hand as he led her from the room.

"Dean, this could have turned out so much worse. I don't know what I would have done if I'd lost them, really lost them."

They were seated on the couch, shoulders and legs touching. Shannon gripped her wine stem tightly and laid her head on Dean's shoulder.

"Don't think about it. They're safe. They're home. We're not going to let anything happen to them … ever." He pressed his lips to her hair, the kiss lingering.

"We?" She took a sip of the dry Chardonnay. Just that morning she'd dared to hope that she could have her own happily ever after. But then he'd told her it was better that they keep their distance.

Dean blew out a gusty sigh that tickled as it made its way down her neck and straight under the ribbed tank top she wore. He set his wine glass down on the coffee table, gently slipping hers from her fingers and placing it beside his own. He twisted on the couch cushion, reaching for Shannon's hands. His thumbs rubbed circles into her knuckles.

"I guess I need to back up a bit, huh?" He waited for her to meet his eyes. The warmth and sincerity she saw there had her leaning closer.

"Maybe a little."

"So, your birthday party ... that I crashed with all of my friends," he began.

"You were invited. I meant to invite you. I should have ..." She dropped her gaze to her lap, chewing on her bottom lip as shame infused her cheeks with a prickly heat.

"Shh ... I'm not done." He placed a finger on her lips for a fleeting moment and brushed a thumb across her cheekbone before taking hold of her hand once again.

"I messed up so bad. I lied about who I was. I created the perfect life here in this little town with you and I was so scared that if I told you who I was, you'd see me differently. I asked my bandmates to help convince you that I wasn't this deadbeat jerk of a celebrity. I figured if you saw how they'd traded fame for family, you could see that I could do it too."

"You sure you didn't invite them out here to reassure yourself that you could become a family man?" She tilted her head to the side, her left brow raised high as she waited for his answer.

"Didn't have to. You showed me that. You and Brady and Brian and that little flirt, Brenna." He squeezed her hands, the love in his eyes squeezing her heart.

"But I thought everything was okay. I was so happy when I woke up this morning. Then the kids told me you didn't even speak to them at the party. They wanted to know what I'd done. Only, I didn't know." Just remembering it made it a little hard to breathe.

"I was so stupid, Shannon. I saw Vince at the party. I wasn't even sure if he was there because you'd gotten back together or not. It didn't matter. I'd convinced myself that he deserved to be their father more than me. He's their biological father, after all. I was trying to be this noble freaking gentleman and back off. Telling you no this morning was the hardest thing I've ever done."

"Oh, Dean." She melted against him, wrapping her arms around his waist and holding on for dear life. After a moment, she raised her head and gave him a watery smile. "I should have explained. Vince wanted to meet them, but on my terms. The kids don't even know he's their father. They thought they were just meeting an old friend of mine. Yeah, it scared the hell out of me when he emailed to announce he was coming to town to visit. I wanted to talk to you about it. But I wasn't speaking to you." She rolled her eyes, disgusted with herself.

"I wish you had."

"Me too." She traced a finger across his knee, grinning at his quick intake of breath. "Vince was here looking for absolution, or something like that. He's getting remarried. He was definitely not here to pick up where we left off." Shannon took a second to sneak in a gulp of wine. She wiped her mouth with the back of her hand, a bright smile in place. "He likes you, you know. I told him how good you are with the triplets. He's happy that they've got such a good male role model."

"I don't need his approval," Dean growled. The hard set of his jaw showed determination, possessiveness.

While it was a tad caveman, Shannon couldn't deny that his reaction was an incredible turn on. She squirmed on the couch, taking another big sip of wine to cool her parched throat.

"Even if I hadn't found you in the parking lot of that produce stand, I intended to come by today. I was going to convince you that I'd make the better dad for those kids. Just because he donated sperm, doesn't make him a father."

"Preaching to the choir, babe." She winked, then sobered. One last question was still bothering her.

"Are you sure you're staying here in Scallop Shores? Won't you miss all the perks that come with living in Southern California?"

"Of course I'm staying here. I'm the new music teacher at the elementary school, remember?" His smile was teasing.

"It's just that, at the party, I heard everyone talking about some reunion special taping in LA. I thought you were going back."

"Yeah, the reunion show. I didn't want to do it, but I promised the guys that if they came out and helped me win you back, I'd do the stupid show ... for them. Tit for tat, ya know? But that'll take a weekend, tops. The kids are going to love the West Coast. Have they ever been on a plane? Oh, we'll have to include Disneyland. Okay, maybe we need more than a weekend."

Shannon set her glass down on the coffee table and turned to Dean, who was still chattering excitedly about all the different theme parks in the Los Angeles area. Her smile was bemused.

"You want us to come with you? All of us?"

"Of course. I'm not going anywhere without you ... all of you. Because we're a family now. Or at least I think of us as a family. I mean, if you want to come with me. I didn't even ask." He wiped sweaty palms on his cargo shorts, his eyes darting between Shannon's face and the wine glass he'd abandoned just inches away.

"You're right. You aren't going anywhere unless we all go—as a family." She traced his rugged jaw with her index finger. "I love you, you know."

"And I love you—all four of you."

More from This Author
(From *Drawn to Jonah* by Jennifer DeCuir)

If bad things really did come in threes, then a flat tire in a chilly October rainstorm rounded out the trifecta. Though a failed marriage and the death of her beloved grandmother certainly put this particular crimp in perspective. Quinn eased her BMW to the shoulder and prayed that she wasn't inviting more trouble by getting the wheels stuck in gooey, back roads mud. She leaned her head against the backrest and closed her eyes.

The engine was idling, the wipers barely able to keep up with the sheet of rain pouring steadily from the sky. Daylight was giving up its last gasp and Quinn was stranded on a road that didn't see much traffic at the best of times. This move back to Scallop Shores, Maine, was not starting off well.

She rooted through the usual plethora of junk in her purse, searching for her elusive cell phone. Of course it hid at the very bottom. Quinn grimaced when her fingers came in contact with something sticky—she didn't want to know. Seconds later, she fished the phone out of her bag. "Yes!"

The battery was dead. "No, no, no!" She threw the phone to the floor, startling the cat in the kennel beside her, still sleepy from kitty-downers. "I just charged this last night." The day officially could not get any worse.

Distracted, she didn't realize she was no longer alone on the quiet rural road until a tall silhouette suddenly loomed at the driver's side window. Grizzabella, the cat, hissed. Quinn screamed. Her heart thudded in time with the thumping on her window as the larger-than-life man tried to get her attention. How had he snuck up on her like that?

She twisted in her seat to look behind her. Sure enough, a large white pickup truck had pulled to the edge of the road, its light color still discernable against the bright autumn wardrobe that dressed the trees lining the road. Squinting, Quinn could make out someone else in the truck.

The city girl in her balked at the idea of opening her window, even an inch, to talk to this man. But the small-town girl, the one raised right here, remembered that folks in Scallop Shores helped each other out. Even if it meant getting a thorough dousing while waiting to do a good deed. She lowered the window.

"Got yourself into a bind, huh? Pop the trunk, I'll get the spare out." He grinned, showing dazzling teeth, and Quinn thought it unfair that one man could have been gifted with so many gorgeous features.

"I can get out. Do you want me to get out? Maybe I could help." Quinn shoved a knuckle into her mouth to stop the blathering.

Raking a large hand through his soggy dark hair, the stranger tossed her an amused stare and shook his head. When she just sat there, he nodded toward the button that would release the trunk. Oh yeah.

Quinn sunk low in her seat, embarrassed that she'd gotten so flustered over a good-looking stranger. He was just a man. She scooted back up and checked out what was going on through the rearview mirror. He hefted out the spare tire and jack and slammed the trunk closed. He really was big. Tall, broad-shouldered, pec muscles clearly defined by the soaked-through T-shirt that clung like a second skin.

Sure her assessment through the rearview mirror had been covert, Quinn nearly squealed when the stranger stopped to stare back at her. Even in the fading twilight, she could see just how icy blue his eyes were. There was nothing icy about the slow heat that spread through her veins when their eyes met.

She squirmed in her seat, trying to ignore this physical reaction that she had no time or use for. Relief flooded through her as she spied her sketchpad on the passenger seat. She snatched it like a lifeline. Switching on the overhead light and flipping to an empty sheet, she braced the little notebook against the bouncing of the car as it was jacked up. Quinn started to draw. She always started with the eyes. What would hers say right now?

Relief. Things hadn't worked out. Marriage wasn't for everyone. Coming back to the small New England town where she was raised was the perfect place to start over. She was better off alone.

Her thoughts wandered until a tap on her window made her jump again. She lowered it just a crack.

"Making sure you'll have a positive ID for the police?" He lowered his gaze to the drawing in her lap. Quinn looked down in horror to see the stranger's face staring back at her.

"I, uh, sketch when I'm bored." She'd meant to say nervous but didn't want him to know how much he'd affected her. She ripped the page out of the book and passed it through the space in the window. "Here, take it."

He took the picture, staring at it curiously.

"I'd really like to give you something for your time." *Oh good lord, could that have come out any more suggestive?* Quinn felt her cheeks grow warm again.

"I was raised not to expect anything for helping someone in need."

"Then I hope to return the favor someday."

He raised an eyebrow. "You're going to change a flat on my truck?" Chuckling, he headed back to his own vehicle.

That wasn't what she'd meant! He had deliberately misunderstood her. Quinn turned around in her seat, but he was already getting into his truck. He pulled up alongside her car and rolled down the passenger side window.

"Have a nice trip."

He'd noticed the New York plates then.

Well, she was done with New York City. She was done with broken dreams. And she was especially done with men. Quinn Baker was starting over—and she was in Scallop Shores to stay.

. . .

Did he really look that cranky? He looked mean. She made him look mean. Jonah threw the sketch back on the kitchen table where he'd been staring at it, off and on, since they got home earlier.

"What do you think, Cuteness? Do I look like a grouch?" He turned to Lily, fresh out of the tub, all pink cheeks and footy PJ's.

"No, silly. You aren't green and you don't live in a trash can." She giggled, referring to a Sesame Street character.

Jonah grabbed his daughter close and tickled her ribs. Hauling her over his shoulder, her shrieks ringing down the hallway, he carried her to her bedroom. He paused in the doorway of the room he had painted pale pink the very day the ultrasound revealed they were having a girl.

He pretended like he was going to set Lily down on the floor, but at the last second, dropped her onto the mattress. This was their nightly routine, and one would think she'd tire of it. Jonah grinned when she laughed breathlessly, and asked for more.

"It's late. Time for a quick story before I send you off to dreamland." He reached for the well-worn copy of *Goodnight Moon* in Lily's book basket.

"No, Daddy, read me the one about the fairies tonight. Please?" She pointed to a picture book with a group of brightly colored fairies on the front.

"Only because you're the cutest little girl I know."

He'd long ago memorized the words to *Goodnight Moon* when Paige had read it to Lily. It was a safe book. This one he had to make up on the spot, and that scared the hell out of him. He took a deep breath and prayed that he told it the same way he had the last time.

It wouldn't be long now. She was a smart kid. Heck, she was almost four already. Jonah couldn't bear to see the look on his precious daughter's face when she learned his secret. Daddies were supposed to know everything.

Lily snuggled under the covers, clutching her stuffed friends. Jonah kissed his daughter goodnight and smiled as she waved goodbye with her teddy bear's paw.

Jonah threw on an extra layer of dry clothes, still chilled after the soaking he'd gotten changing a tire for the woman stranded out on Rangeley Way. He couldn't get her out of his head.

She'd been driving the latest model BMW. Though evening had been setting in, he'd still been able to see that her outfit looked like something straight off a boutique store mannequin. A fitted wool jacket, tall leather boots (oh, yeah, he'd noticed how high those went!) and brand-new jeans that still had a crease down the middle.

She'd taken perfectly nice honey-blonde hair and had those professional highlights painted on to make it blonder. He couldn't understand why women did that to themselves. Waste of good money, if you asked him.

So why was it that she looked so "city" and still seemed "small-town" approachable? Unbidden, Jonah suddenly pictured her in one of his old plaid, flannel shirts and nothing else. She'd have her fancy hair all piled up on her head, and her bare toes painted some ultra-feminine shade of pink. *Whoa! Down boy!* It wasn't like him to react so physically to a stranger he happened to meet on the road.

Refocusing the direction of his thoughts, Jonah felt a pang of guilt. Lots of tourists missed the turnoff to the highway and ended up lost out on those back roads. He should have offered that woman directions. Wait, what was he thinking? He hadn't noticed it, but surely a fancy car like that would have state-of-the-art GPS.

Frowning over how much time he was spending obsessing over soft brown eyes and lush curves, he shook the woman from his thoughts and headed down to his workshop.

He'd lived his whole life in this house and had learned woodworking beside his father as soon as he'd been old enough to safely wield the tools. They had started out making birdhouses and spice racks, the usual father/son woodworking stuff. Then as his skill set grew, his dad had taught him how to make furniture.

Jonah wished his dad were still alive. He'd love to be able to show him how he'd improved on some of the basic designs they had worked on together. He liked experimenting with the lathe, creating more and more intricate designs.

Tonight he had some sanding to do on a cradle he was making for the neighbors across the road. Ken and Thea were having their first baby in January. Thea had seen some of his previous work and gushed over the detailing. He hoped they hadn't bought a cradle yet, because this was going to be a gift from him and Lily.

Settling down on the cold cement floor, Jonah winced, thinking he should have brought down a nice, hot cup of coffee. He drew the cradle onto his lap as best he could, and gently began to buff the surface smooth. If he had a wife, she could sew a nice quilt to go inside. Now that would make a fine gift.

If he had a wife. He'd been thinking about that a lot lately. Not the wife part, really, but a mother for Lily. The older his daughter got, the more out of his element Jonah felt. Lily wasn't a baby anymore. Now she wanted her hair braided, she wanted to wear fairy costumes, girl things that he didn't have the first clue about. She needed a woman's influence.

But before he could convince someone to take them on and be a mother for Lily, he had to learn to read. Pure luck had allowed him to skate through life so far. The only person in his adult life that had figured out what he kept hidden from the world was his wife, Paige. She'd taken his secret to the grave.

In the mood for more Crimson Romance?
Check out *Valentine Vote* by Susan Blexrud
at *CrimsonRomance.com*.

www.ingramcontent.com/pod-product-compliance
Lightning Source LLC
Chambersburg PA
CBHW010638100726
47900CB00011B/2875